"What makes you think I kept those letters?"

"Oh, you got rid of them?" Patrick said, leaping to the wrong conclusion.

Elinor didn't correct him. Pride kept her from telling the truth, that she'd treasured them over the years, unwilling to sever the last link to Patrick. She was also curious to hear what he'd say next.

"Firth had a long talk with me when he asked me if I was interested in running," he explained. "He quizzed me all about my past—the usual things that come up to smear a candidate. Cheating on exams, drugs, criminal record, sex."

"I thought we were talking about love."

"You know what I mean."

"Cheating and drugs and crime—funny, I wouldn't have included love in that list, myself."

"You're right, of course. Love belongs in a list with moonbeams and orchids...and Elinor Waring."

Dear Reader,

Welcome to Silhouette—experience the magic of the wonderful world where two people fall in love. Meet heroines that will make you cheer for their happiness, and heroes (be they the boy next door or a handsome, mysterious stranger) who will win your heart. Silhouette Romance reflects the magic of love—sweeping you away with books that will make you laugh and cry, heartwarming, poignant stories that will move you time and time again.

In the coming months we're publishing romances by many of your all-time favorites, such as Diana Palmer, Brittany Young, Sondra Stanford and Annette Broadrick. Your response to these authors and our other Silhouette Romance authors has served as a touchstone for us, and we're pleased to bring you more books with Silhouette's distinctive medley of charm, wit and—above all—*romance*.

I hope you enjoy this book and the many stories to come. Experience the magic!

Sincerely,

Tara Hughes
Senior Editor
Silhouette Books

JOAN SMITH

Maybe Next Time

Silhouette *Romance*

Published by Silhouette Books New York
America's Publisher of Contemporary Romance

SILHOUETTE BOOKS
300 E. 42nd St., New York, N.Y. 10017

ISBN: 0-373-08635-0

First Silhouette Books printing March 1989

Printed in the U.S.A.

Books by Joan Smith

Silhouette Romance

Next Year's Blonde #234
Caprice #255
From Now On #269
Chance of a Lifetime #288
Best of Enemies #302
Trouble in Paradise #315
Future Perfect #325
Tender Takeover #343
The Yielding Art #354
The Infamous Madam X #430
Where There's a Will #452
Dear Corrie #546
If You Love Me #562
By Hook or By Crook #591
After the Storm #617
Maybe Next Time #635

JOAN SMITH

has written many Regency romances, but likes working with the greater freedom of contemporaries. She also enjoys mysteries and Gothics, collects Japanese porcelain and is a passionate gardener. A native of Canada, she is the mother of three.

DELTA, A FICTITIOUS CITY IN THE FINGER LAKES DISTRICT OF NEW YORK

Gordon's house

WHYM TV Station

Delta Arms Hotel

Trattoria Vespucci

Main Street

Plant Shed

Coffee Shop

Maple Drive

Maple Drive Apartments, where Elinor lives

Chapter One

Outside, snow swirled in lacy curtains of white in the black velvet air. The flakes sparkled like diamond chips in the illumination of the street lamps. Elinor Waring took one last, admiring look through the window before drawing the drapes and turning back to the tropical oasis of her living room.

She loved plants in any season, but their company was especially welcome when the snow flew and all the natural vegetation was in deep freeze for the winter. A row of large jade plants sat in a flower box in front of the window. Nothing seemed to affect these hardy friends. Not the warm blast from the radiator, nor the cooler wind that seeped in around the balcony door. Nearby, the swaying fronds of a Madagascar dragon tree seemed equally impervious to adverse conditions.

Too bad she couldn't convince more of her customers to try these simple plants, Elinor thought. It would be a change from the endless profusion of *Ficus benjamina* and palms that everyone wanted. Not that she had anything against the ficus and palms! Plants of any sort were not only her livelihood but her passion. Elinor owned and operated The Plant Shed. She had begun her enterprise in a glassed-in shed behind Raleigh's Fashion Shoppe. Three years later, when business had picked up, she had moved across the street into a regular store, but she'd kept the more modest name.

Her spraying and watering done, Elinor turned off the grow lights, because plants needed rest, like people. Next she plugged in the Christmas tree bulbs, and the small spruce in the corner leaped into multicolored life. Beneath it lay a pile of brightly wrapped Christmas presents in readiness for the big day. She breathed in the scent of resin and needles that carried evanescent memories of Christmases past, at home on the farm.

She idly picked up the TV guide and scanned it. Too late for her favorite sitcom and too early for the news. She was saturated with police dramas and decided to watch the public television show on orchids that she'd taped on the weekend. Just as she was rewinding the tape, there was a knock at her door.

She wasn't surprised to see her neighbor, Gillie Parson, nor was she much surprised to see that Gillie held a wilting fern in her hands.

"Help!" Gillie said. "I feel like a plant murderess. Me and my brown thumb. This is the third fern I've killed this year."

Gillie certainly didn't look like a murderess. Her ruler-straight bobbed hair framed a pixie face. Her big green eyes wore the innocent luster of youth. In her oversize jersey and jeans she looked like a kid, which was probably why her children's show on the local television channel was so popular. The audience identified with her.

"What weapon did you use this time?" Elinor asked, taking the fern and examining it. She knew by the weight of the flimsy plastic pot that it was heavy with water. "Hmm, death by drowning, I'd say. Maybe we can resuscitate it, if it's not too late."

They went together to the miniature kitchen. A small refrigerator, a stove, a table and two chairs filled the floor space. Even Elinor's inventiveness couldn't find room for her beloved plants anywhere except on the windowsills. There, small pots of parsley and oregano flourished. She took the fern to the sink and turned it upside down, watching in dismay as a cup of murky water poured out. She cast an accusing eye on her friend.

Gillie smiled guiltily. "You said I should try to follow its natural habitat," Gillie reminded her. "Ferns grow in damp, shady places, so I kept it well watered and in the dark—sort of. In a corner."

"Damp, not doused," Elinor pointed out. "And a clay pot would be better, to let the poor thing breathe. I'll repot it for you, but the roots are probably rotted. And incidentally, you don't have to keep it that dark.

Ferns are really hard to grow, Gillie. Did you ever think of trying a jade?"

"Trying to find a home for another of your orphans, huh?" Gillie said knowingly.

"That's the idea. I never can throw out a living plant, and every leaf that falls sprouts into another plant. Want some coffee?"

"Yes, please, but that's not why I came over. I was wondering if you'd be a guest on my *Miss Gillie Show*—again. The kids always like your guest spots."

"Sure. When? And who canceled this time?"

"Wednesday. Sorry for the short notice. I had a dentist booked but she's in the hospital with appendicitis. She was supposed to show the kids how to floss. Thanks, Ellie. I really appreciate it. Maybe you could do something Christmassy. You know, like poinsettias, the way you put them in your closet in the fall so they'll bloom for Christmas."

"That's too complicated for children. I gave up on that myself. How about Christmas cactus?"

Gillie nodded. "Christmas cactus would be good."

"And a few minutes on the result of overwatering *any* plant," Elinor added, looking at the wilting fern on her counter. "It's known as killing with kindness."

They took their coffee into the living room. "Mind if we watch WHYM?" Gillie asked. "Luke's interviewing Congressman Firth." Luke Williams was Gillie's boyfriend and co-worker at the local television station.

"Is Firth in town for the bankers' convention or the closing of the bicentennial celebration?" Elinor asked.

"For the publicity," Gillie said, and laughed. "He wouldn't pass up an opportunity like this. Luke says he's planning to run for the Senate next year. Delta's his hometown, and the excuse for this visit is the town's bicentennial, but he wouldn't be spending a whole week here if it weren't for the national coverage the bankers are getting. The networks have all got reporters here for the convention."

They settled in to watch the interview. Congressman Firth was the guest speaker at the Delta Chamber of Commerce dinner. The dinner was over, and Luke was conducting an informal interview in a quiet corner of the hotel ballroom. It still surprised Elinor that sober, serious Luke Williams, who looked like a professor in his dark-rimmed glasses, had fallen in love with more flamboyant Gillie.

The interview soon turned into a speech of the predictable sort, with Firth praising the industry and character of Delta's inhabitants and insinuating that the city's prosperity was inextricably linked to the election of its incumbent congressman.

Gillie pointed at a man hovering just behind Congressman Firth. "That's Tony Gower. Luke says he's the one that will probably replace Firth when he moves to the Upper House. He's already his assistant or secretary or something."

Elinor wasn't listening. She had spotted a more interesting face on Firth's other side. It looked like—no, it couldn't be. She was imagining things. Patrick Barron was a lawyer. He had nothing to do with politics. But the resemblance was striking enough to send her heart hammering in her throat.

Patrick Barron. Lord, how long had it been? Three years, four? No, three and a half. She had come within a breath of marrying him. They had even gone looking for engagement rings. Elinor always thought that in an odd way, the high price of diamonds had prevented their marriage. Patrick had just finished law school and had been offered a good job by a firm in New York. Then a job that paid much less but that he wanted to take had come along with a civil rights organization in Washington, D.C. She remembered their discussion about his decision as if it had occurred yesterday.

"The trouble is, the salary will hardly support *one*, let alone two," he had said. Concern had etched lines in his forehead and shadowed his eyes. "And I promised you that little solitaire like your mother's."

"I don't have to have an engagement ring. Really, it doesn't mean that much to me. And you don't have to support me. I'll be working, too, Patrick, making money. I can help."

"No, you want to start your flower shop."

"*Nursery!* I don't just want to *sell* plants. I want to *grow* them."

"That will be all the more expensive, hiring or building a greenhouse. A new business always loses money at first, Ellie. I told you I'd help you get started. I'll take the job in New York. Later, when we've saved up, I'll go with the civil rights organization."

His generous offer had been sincerely made, but she could see how hard it had been for him. And why had he applied for the civil rights job in the first place if he hadn't intended to take it? He must have had some idea what it paid. "No, I'll work for someone else first, one of the established nurseries," she had insisted. "I still have lots to learn."

"I can't ask you to do that."

"I can't ask you to take a job you don't want, either."

She had known how badly Patrick wanted that poorer-paying job. He had wanted it with the same fervor she felt for plants. In the end, they had had a fight and broken up because they were both too stubborn and too determined not to let the other make the sacrifice. A new reason for breaking up: an excess of love.

Or had it been more complicated than that? In retrospect, Elinor wondered if either of them had really wanted to go through with the wedding. Maybe they had both been too young, not really ready for the responsibilities of marriage. They had both used the other's potential sacrifice as an excuse to break off their relationship. After all, Patrick *had* applied for that civil rights job. Although he'd claimed that one of his professors had recommended him and that he had gone to the interview out of curiosity, he did want that job. So Elinor had pointed out reasonably that the time to start her business was before assuming those responsibilities, and Patrick had agreed.

Patrick had taken the job in Washington, and Elinor had opened her nursery in Delta, in lower New York, just ten miles from her family farm. They hadn't kept in touch. Not a phone call, not a letter. They would have kept in touch if it had been real love, wouldn't they? Ellie felt it was better that way. She had soon become totally absorbed in her business, and she assumed Patrick had done the same.

Meanwhile the camera had moved away from the man on the screen, but it didn't matter. She still saw him in her mind's eye, where his image was printed indelibly. One quick flash was enough to trigger the memory labeled Patrick Barron, which was still vividly alive after three and a half years. Straight jet black hair, tinged with blue under light. Eyes a deep, marine blue that turned nearly black when he was angry and glowed with passion when he was excited. A strong, mannish, well-shaped nose. An ascetically lean but strong face, with high cheekbones and a square, determined jaw. If it weren't for his generous, slightly crooked lips, he would look awfully stubborn. That mouth betrayed his roguish sense of humor.

"What's so funny?" Gillie asked, calling her back to attention.

"Nothing." Elinor focused on the screen and noticed the interview was over. She had missed nine-tenths of it.

"Don't you think he's handsome?" Gillie said in an impatient way that told Elinor she had asked the question before.

"Oh, yes, very handsome!"

"A little young, of course."

"He must be nearly thirty by now," Elinor murmured vaguely.

"More like thirty-seven or -eight, I'd say. You only have to be twenty-five to run, but the candidates are usually older."

Elinor blinked. "Candidates for what?"

"For what we're talking about, Ellie. Make that what *I'm* talking about. I have the feeling your mind's in the kitchen with that dead fern. I said Tony Gower will probably be the candidate to replace Congressman Firth in the next election for the House of Representatives. The party's golden-haired boy, Luke tells me. Who did you think I meant?"

"I—I thought I recognized someone in the crowd. I'm probably mistaken, but I was thinking of him."

"What's his name?"

"Patrick Barron." How odd it seemed, to hear those familiar words on her tongue. She said them reluctantly, as if they still had some power to hurt her.

Gillie looked sharply. "What did he do, jilt you or something? You don't look too happy."

"I used to go out with him," Elinor said vaguely. As close as she was to Gillie, she had never discussed that particular episode in any detail. She had never even told Gillie his name, though Gillie knew there was a significant man in her past.

"Don't tell me he's the man you were engaged to at college! The one you don't talk about!"

"There's nothing to talk about," Elinor said swiftly. "We just decided not to get married, that's all."

Gillie looked at her skeptically. "But is that him— Patrick Barron?"

"Yes," Elinor said diffidently.

"Sounds like unfinished business to me."

"Don't be silly. It was all tied up years ago."

Gillie hunched her shoulders, unconvinced. "If he's the one I think you're talking about, he certainly is handsome. I wouldn't be in any hurry to break off with a man like that, but if you say so... Luke's calling me after the interview. I better dash. I'll check up on my fern soon. And you won't forget the guest spot on Wednesday? Christmas cactus."

"Right, and the lethal effects of overwatering."

"It looked thirsty. I let the last one die of neglect, if you remember."

"This one was gasping for air in that aquarium you provided."

"Maybe I should get a fish, huh? Thanks for the coffee."

Gillie let herself out, and Elinor turned down the TV volume while her mind reverted to the past. What would a civil rights lawyer be doing at Delta's bicentennial celebration? What would Patrick be doing with Congressman Firth?

Even as she considered this, the TV camera, at the ball now, panned the room. She saw a form that made her sit bolt upright. It *was* Patrick! She recognized the lean, elegant body, the graceful way he danced. There was no mistaking that smooth black hair. She peered more closely to try to see the woman with him, but all she saw was a wave of blond hair over his shoulder before the camera moved away again.

Elinor shrugged her shoulders, pretending not to care. So what if it was him? He had to be somewhere. Maybe the woman with him was some relation to Congressman Firth. He had two daughters, whose faces often appeared in the local paper. One of them had silky blond hair. Elinor knew Patrick's job put him in contact with lots of politicians. He could hardly live in Washington and not know some of them. But why was he *here*? Was he going with one of Firth's daughters? It must be serious if he was tagging along on this visit home. A wince of jealousy pricked at her. Jealousy, after all this time? She must be crazy.

She rose, turned off the set and went purposefully to the kitchen to tend to the sodden fern. It slipped easily out of the pot. She carefully pressed the excess water out of its roots. They were soft but not mushy. The rot hadn't set in yet. Maybe the fern would recover if she dried the roots well and repotted it with some dry earth to soak up the excess water. She'd put it in an earthenware pot and not water it for a while.

As she worked, Elinor mentally compared plant life to human life. Killing with kindness, she had said to Gillie, and in a way, she and Patrick had killed their romance with kindness. They had doused each other with so much concern that the relationship expired. Too bad she couldn't just repot the affair and start over.

Elinor laid newspapers on the counter. From under the sink she got out a bag of potting soil and an empty pot. Her hands were deep in moist earth when the phone rang. She grabbed a paper towel and used it to protect the phone.

"Hello."

"Ellie? It's Patrick."

His voice came like a ghost from the past, jarring her with memories. It was a firm, resonant voice, with a lyrical lilt carried down the generations from his Irish ancestors. An authoritative voice that she always thought would suit a lawyer, but it could soften, too, at the right moment. It was soft now, but with uncertainty. "Patrick Barron," he added. "Is this Elinor Waring?"

Her breath caught in her lungs and he repeated the question. "Yes! Yes, it's me. Patrick, what are you doing here?"

"At the moment I'm at the Delta Arms Hotel, trying to make a date to see you. Glad to hear it's still Ms. Waring and not Mrs. Somebody. Are you busy?"

"I—" Her instinct was to invite him over. But she held back because despite her first pleased reaction, there was definitely a strong feeling of reluctance to see him. The opposing forces warred in her until she convinced herself she was being unreasonable. He wasn't going to bite her or force her to marry him.

"No, not terribly busy. When did you have in mind?" She hastily checked her calendar. The next evening was a perfect blank.

"I thought you might like to come over here to the hotel."

"Now?"

"As soon as possible. There's a very good party going on. I was hoping you'd be here."

She didn't want him to think she was unpopular. "No, I decided against it. There are so many parties on this season," she said vaguely. In the middle of December, there were plenty of days on her calendar carrying reminders of parties.

"If you're free, why don't you slip into something festive and come over? Don't worry about a ticket. I'll meet you at the door. Or I can pick you up, if you'll tell me how to get to your place."

"No, that's not necessary. It's just that—well, it's short notice and rather late," she said. But a peek at her watch told her it was only nine-thirty.

"Late? The party's just beginning." He laughed nervously, and when he spoke again, his voice was lower, intimate, coaxing. "It's been such a long time. I'd really like to see you, Ellie. I won't be in town long."

His words finally made up Elinor's mind. Patrick was probably here only for the day, and heaven knew when she'd have a chance to see him again. It would be fun to renew their—she mentally hesitated over the word—friendship. It had been more than that, but affair didn't quite cover it, either. Romance. That was the word she was looking for, and renewing it was out of the question. What might be wise, however, was to kill off the memories, once and for all.

"All right. I'll throw something on and go over."

"Bless your kind heart. I'll be waiting—*very* impatiently." His voice was a caress and a promise.

Elinor hung up the receiver and stared at her muddied fingers. They were trembling. Her whole body was trembling with anticipation and something less pleasant, which might possibly be apprehension. Was she being a fool?

She put the newly potted fern on the windowsill between two pots of parsley, rolled the newspaper up in a ball and disposed of it while she mulled over what she'd wear. Patrick had been wearing a formal black jacket when she saw him on TV. It was a ball, after all, not just a party, so she'd have to wear something special.

Anticipation lent a glow to her complexion as she prepared. The deep blue gown she slid on had been bought for an upcoming New Year's Eve party. It was a low-cut, sophisticated design that clung to the swell of her breasts and nipped in to show her slender waist. The bottom of the skirt ballooned out flirtatiously. The somberness of the color was lightened by a vibrant silk shawl and gold sandals.

She hadn't worn clothes like this during her relationship with Patrick. As far as she knew, he hadn't even *owned* an evening jacket in those days, only jeans and cords and sweaters. How vividly the images danced in her head. Would he think she had changed much? She used to wear her chestnut hair short, but she hadn't had much more than a trim in three years, and now loose, layered waves circled her face.

In the mirror she could see that the lamplight painted coppery highlights when she moved her head. Her eyes, wide spaced, a stormy gray edged in long lashes, were her best feature. She applied silver eye shadow with a light touch and stood back to view the effect. She smiled with satisfaction and in a way that removed any air of sophistication. That youthful smile betrayed the young romantic hiding beneath the worldly veneer.

It was a nuisance to struggle into snow boots, but she couldn't wear sandals in the snow. Elinor drove her white nursery van, with the words The Plant Shed emblazoned on the side. She had wanted a painting of a plant there, too. Unfortunately the artist had executed the philodendron so badly that it looked like a misbegotten weed, so she'd had it removed. Although the business was doing well, she hadn't yet graduated to a personal car. The van served a dual purpose, and she had to be careful of dirtying her coat.

She drove slowly through the swirling spirals of snow. It wasn't a major storm, more of a playful prank by Mother Nature, but it made driving tricky. The snow had come early this year. Already it was piled in drifts on the side streets, waiting to be hauled away.

The hotel had underground parking, so Elinor put on her sandals before she went inside. As she took the elevator upstairs, her stomach felt queasy. She told herself it was just the effect of the sudden rise in elevation. Why on earth should she feel sick with excitement at the thought of seeing Patrick Barron again? It was just a friendly visit for old times' sake. That's all it was.

Chapter Two

When Patrick said he'd be waiting for her at the door, she had thought he meant the *ballroom* door, but he was at the door to the street, peering out. Coming into the lobby from the parking lot elevator, Elinor spotted him before he saw her, and she noticed with a sense of gratification that he was as nervous as she was. While she checked her coat, she watched him. He frequently glanced at his watch, peered out at the arriving cars, then paced like an expectant father before repeating the performance. A few passing women turned to take a second look at him.

Patrick had always worn his devastating good looks with an air of insouciance. He had an innate elegance that had made him look superb even when he wore a corduroy jacket and sweater with jeans. In a black jacket and white tie, he was enough to take her breath away. How had she let him go? The question popped unbidden into her head, and she couldn't find a satisfactory answer. Sheer stupidity, she decided. That's what it had been. She wasn't so frivolous that she'd been bowled over by only his looks and charm. There had been a real strength of character there, as well. His choice of career testified to that. He was the kind of man she hoped to marry one day; the timing just hadn't been right. But she was older now, more mature. Maybe this time...

Then he turned and saw her. She's changed! was the first idea that struck him. Then he noticed that she was even more beautiful than he remembered. Young Ellie had grown into a glamorous woman. That svelte gown didn't leave much doubt as to her size and shape. When he thought of her, and he often did, he thought of her with a dirty face and her hands in earth, tending some invalid plant. An unconscious little frown pleated his brow as he came forward.

Then she smiled, and the feeling of strangeness evaporated. Ellie always had a magic smile. Her eyes danced, and her lips wobbled. They were wobbling now. He felt he had been catapulted back three years. Without a word of greeting, they both gave a nervous laugh and wrapped their arms around each other and held on tight for a long minute. After this warm bear hug, they both stood back and smiled.

"Patrick! It was such a surprise to hear from you."

"I was afraid I'd got the wrong number. You didn't recognize my voice. I hardly recognized *you* when I first saw you. Very nice, by the way." His dark eyes did a quick, appreciative survey.

She flushed with pleasure. "It's new. Actually I'm cheating. This was supposed to be a Christmas present to myself, to wear to a New Year's ball."

"That's a Christmas present to whoever your escort is?" His voice rose slightly at the end, making it a question. If she says she's engaged, he thought, I don't know how I'll feel. But that was what he had expected, wasn't it? Even what he wanted. This was no time for him to get seriously tied up with a woman. A fiancé would remove that danger. And he realized, as he gazed at her, that there was danger in seeing much more of Ellie.

Elinor ignored the implied question. She didn't have a New Year's date yet, though she had two or three possibles lined up. "What are you doing in Delta?"

"Shall we find a quiet corner and talk before we dance? There must be a bar somewhere." He wanted just a quick drink. He could hardly blurt out his request immediately. There were three and a half years of indifference to be talked away first, and really he wanted to hear all about her present life.

They walked down the lobby until they found a small, dark bar that was nearly deserted. The strains of music from the ballroom echoed around them. The seating arrangement was formal, which was all to the good. He should stay out of intimate dark corners with Ellie.

"I thought I saw you on TV, just before you called," Elinor said. "Are you here with Congressman Firth or the bankers?"

"Me, a banker?" He laughed. "You seem to forget, I never got hung up over money." He'd get the catching-up business over with as quickly as possible and get right down to the favor he had to ask. He was uncomfortable with it, but it had to be done.

"I'm working with Firth now. The civil rights group disbanded for lack of funds. Firth was one of our staunchest supporters, and he hired me to work for him. I've been researching subsidized housing for the underprivileged, up until now."

"So you're in politics, sort of?"

He eagerly took up this safe subject. "I'm getting in deeper by the minute. I never saw my career taking this path, but in the end it's politics that makes any improvement possible. Why stand outside and beg, when you can go inside and work more effectively?"

They ordered and settled in for a talk. "How about you, Ellie? I don't think you're mucking around with plants in an outfit like that. What are you doing these days? Besides driving the men of Delta wild," he added with a grin. Not one of his eye-gleaming smiles but a grin that robbed the compliment of seriousness.

"Mucking around with plants. I don't usually go formal at work." It was impossible to tell in the shadowy bar, but she thought he looked pleased to hear she was still at the same job.

"Did you ever manage to open your nursery?"

"I certainly did. I have an acre under glass on my dad's farm and my own retail outlet in Delta. I do most of the local greenery business, including the plants in this hotel. I grow the nonflowering plants myself and buy cut blooms and seasonal flowering plants wholesale. This is a very busy season for me. I've sold a thousand poinsettias already and have another shipment coming in tomorrow," she said proudly.

He noticed she still glowed all over when she talked about her plants. He was happy to see her enthusiasm hadn't waned. He squeezed her fingers. "Good for you! I'm delighted you made it."

"I've just begun. I plan to expand my greenhouses this year—double the size. I guess you've found your way, too? Is this what you like, politics?"

He considered the question. "It's a love-hate relationship. Some aspects of it are less than uplifting, but if you want to get things done, you have to have some power."

Elinor listened, frowning. "Doesn't the real power lie in the elected representatives?"

"Precisely." He leaned forward and spoke in a businesslike voice, unaware that his whole body revealed enthusiasm. He was eager to tell her about the brilliant future that awaited him. He acknowledged ruefully that what he really wanted was to impress her. "This isn't for public consumption, but you're looking at the next candidate for representative for this congressional district."

Elinor's eyes widened in surprise. "I heard Firth's resigning, but I understand Tony Gower was the party's choice."

"He was—till very recently. Something has come up. I can't talk about it, but last week Firth asked me if I'd be interested in standing. It isn't certain that I'd win the election, though this district does usually go Democratic. It isn't even certain I'll get the party's nomination, but I have Firth's backing, and of course he's extremely influential.''

"That's wonderful, Patrick. So exciting.''

"He suggested I tag along on this outing. Plenty of media coverage. I'm not a household name, and he feels I need to be seen. Quite frankly, this sort of thing is one of the aspects of the job that doesn't thrill me, but you have to take the bad with the good.''

Elinor looked at him and felt herself choke up with pride. "You'd be a good politician, Patrick. You really *do* care about people. So many politicians don't, nowadays. They seem more interested in advancing their own careers.''

A glow of pleasure warmed Patrick. To bathe in Elinor's approval was better than a Christmas present. "I fought it for quite a while. I don't much care for all the trappings, but Congress is where it happens.''

"You might even be president one day!''

He threw his head back and laughed. "First I have to get elected to Congress. And even before that, I have to get the party's nomination for candidate.''

"I bet you will! I'll help, if I can.''

He squeezed her fingers and smiled intimately. Strike while the iron's hot, he thought. "You can. I have a favor to ask.''

"Ask away!''

Instinct told him her approval would dwindle when she heard why he was here. It would be better to chat a while longer, maybe even dance. It had been so long since he'd held Ellie in his arms. "First let's dance. It's been such a long time....'' Now that they were together again, he was sure Ellie would be willing to help him.

They went into the ballroom. The orchestra was playing a waltz, and Elinor let Patrick draw her into his arms. It felt strange at first, being in his arms again. The reeling rhythm whirled in her head like champagne as they spun around the crowded floor. Patrick's natural sense of rhythm and graceful movements beguiled her. Just a little over an hour ago she had been watching him dance with a blonde on TV, and now she was in his arms. She felt as if she belonged there, and the way he gazed down at her, his eyes half-glazed and dreamy, made her think he felt the same way.

The arm around her waist tightened, drawing her close against him. His chest was a warm haven. Their thighs brushed, soft and intimate as mating butterflies, as they moved to the waltz. A tingle invaded her when he lowered his head and gazed deeply into her eyes.

"Have you missed me?" His voice was husky with memory. The question popped out, unplanned. He shouldn't have said that. It was too intimate—and too revealing, because he really *did* want to hear her answer.

A whole host of memories swarmed over Elinor. Strangely, it was those long walks through the snow that she remembered most vividly. Patrick hadn't had a car in those days so they used to walk, kicking up snow and laughing. Always laughing. Patrick refused to wear a hat. The snow used to settle on his dark hair, glittering like stardust. When they stole kisses, his face was ice-cold but the kisses were warm.

"Of course. Doesn't everyone miss absent friends?" she replied lightly.

He thought her glowing eyes told a different story. Why had he ever let this enchanting woman escape? It had been a gross mistake, and unfortunately this wasn't the time to correct it. He was so busy he hardly had time to get his hair cut, let alone resume a romance that would occupy too much of his time and much, much too much of his thoughts.

He quirked his head and said, "I had the feeling when I called that you didn't want to see me. Are you going with someone now, Ellie?"

She noticed the gleam of avid interest and said, "No one special. I date, of course. How about you?"

"Same thing. My work keeps me very busy, but I see a few women, from time to time. It's hard to establish a serious relationship when I do quite a bit of traveling."

That's all he said, but she read into it a suggestion that it would be easier, and better, to resume an old relationship than to institute a new one. The message was there, in the eyes that studied her as though mesmerized. It was reflected in the lips that had worn a smile ever since she and Patrick had met in the lobby.

"Do you come this way often?" she asked. "Since it's Firth's hometown, I thought maybe—"

"This is the first time I've been here, actually. I hope it won't be the last," he added, with a meaningful look. Now why the devil had he said that? It had slipped out, prompted by a subconscious desire. He'd have to keep his guard up.

Elinor felt sure enough of herself to say, "Why don't you look me up, then? I don't often get to Washington. In fact, I haven't been there for over five years."

"It's not that far away. Only about three hundred miles. If you flew, you could be there in an hour." This was a possibility. It would be nice to see Ellie again.

"Yes," she said, but doubtfully. What am I doing? she thought. Everything is becoming more impossible than ever. I'm securely settled in Delta now. My business is here. Patrick's just moving into a high-powered career in Washington. We could only have fleeting meetings. . . . And why am I worrying about any of this? All he suggested is that I visit him sometime. "I should go and see the cherry blossoms next year."

He was surprised at her lukewarm answer. It didn't seem he had to worry about her getting too serious too soon. "Such enthusiasm!" He laughed, but there was an edge of annoyance there, too. "That isn't till the spring. You should come and see the Christmas trees decorated. And me," he added, holding her gaze for a heart-stopping moment. "I'm told I look dazzling in tinsel and lights."

A spontaneous laugh rippled from her throat, breaking the tension that had begun to build between them. "And a star on top of your head, or do you prefer an angel?"

"You know I've always preferred angels," he said softly, and squeezed her fingers.

As the music ended, they strolled out to the lobby. An empty sofa and some chairs arranged around a big table lured them off to a corner. Elinor sat on the closest chair, then rather regretted it because Patrick couldn't sit right beside her. Neither of them saw the woman approaching. If Elinor had seen her, she would have taken her for a hotel employee. She wore a dark business suit, a white shirt and a man's tie. She was attractive in a crisp sort of way. Short brown hair was brushed back from a high forehead, and she wore a pair of dark-rimmed glasses. When she stopped beside them, Elinor noticed she was carrying a pad and pencil.

Patrick looked up and exclaimed, "Jane! I thought you'd left." He began to struggle out of the sofa.

"Don't get up," the woman said. "Me, leave before the party's over? You know me better than that, Barron."

That the woman had called Patrick by his last name confused Elinor. He had called her Jane. What was the relationship between them? Elinor wondered.

"Mind if I join you?" the woman asked, and sat down before anyone had time to answer. She sat beside Patrick, who moved over to make room with every appearance of pleasure. It was Elinor who felt a spurt of injury at the intrusion.

The woman examined Elinor closely, then gave an arch smile at Patrick. "Where are your manners, Barron? You haven't introduced me to your friend."

"Ms. Waring," he said, and added to Elinor, "This is Ms. Eliot, from the *Washington Journal*."

"Oh, you're a reporter!" Elinor exclaimed, relieved. Of course Patrick would have to be friendly to the press.

Jane Eliot smiled and said, "I'm covering the bankers' convention. Why they chose to hold an international financial convention in limbo is still unclear to me. Of course it's obvious why Firth chose to visit his district at this time."

"Yes, Christmas is a family time," Patrick said. He and Jane exchanged a knowing look.

"And any time is a good time to smile for the TV cameras. But of course I don't have to tell an old trooper like you that," Jane replied archly.

"I'm just a raw recruit," Patrick said.

"You're maturing quickly—and nicely. The cameras love you, by the way. I caught you on Firth's interview this afternoon. Have you got anything quotable to say about this convention?"

"They chose a lovely spot for it," he replied.

"That shouldn't offend anyone, at least."

"I'm serious! You should drive around the area someday, Jane. The Finger Lakes, the southern tier of hills. And the tourist facilities aren't crowded at this time of year, either."

"The bankers aren't here to view the scenery. I expect Firth pulled a few strings to jack up the local economy," Jane said.

Patrick grinned. "They had to hold the convention somewhere. Would you have said the New York City reps had pulled strings if it had been held there?"

Elinor felt she was out of it, as if she was an audience for their repartee.

"Oh, no. That's the logical place. I never question logic." Jane smiled. Then she turned her attention to Elinor. "Do you live here, Miss Waring?"

"Yes. My family has a farm a few miles away."

"And what do you do in the city? Your job, I mean?"

Elinor explained a little about her nursery and flower shop. Jane nodded. She seemed really interested. Her next question was, "Are you active in politics?"

"Not very, but I'm interested. I try to keep myself informed."

"But you're mainly interested in Mr. Barron, I take it?"

Patrick grinned again, at Ms. Eliot. "You can take the Fifth Amendment on that, Ellie," he said.

"Mr. Barron and I are old friends," Elinor replied coolly. A friendly interest was fine, but her personal life was none of the woman's business.

"You're not engaged, I see," Jane remarked, glancing at Elinor's left hand.

Jane returned the examination. "Nor you, Miss Eliot."

The woman laughed. "Oh, no one's interested in *me*. But people would like to know something about the woman in Barron's life. I expect Firth suggested an attractive wife would be a helpful adjunct to a congressman, eh, Barron?"

Elinor hardly knew what to think of this. She was torn between annoyance and curiosity. The thought flashed through her mind that Patrick planned to propose to her. He had mentioned a favor he wanted to ask. But if it was only because he needed an attractive wife to stand beside him during photo sessions, he could take his devastating eyes and his crooked smile back to Washington.

Patrick's smile thinned, and his voice, when he replied, was cool. "Miss Waring and I are just old friends, Jane. I'd appreciate it if you keep her out of this."

"Out of what?" Elinor demanded.

Jane looked surprised. "Didn't you tell her?" She turned back to Elinor. "I'm doing a profile article on Barron. A very complimentary one, I might add, so you can relax your vigilance, Miss Waring. I happen to feel Gower's not the kind of man we want in politics. We've had enough of his sort lately."

"What sort is that?" Elinor asked.

"The man's a womanizer and a foulmouthed scoundrel, in my opinion," Jane said bluntly. "If he didn't have Joe Drury running around to clean up his messes, Firth would have known about it long ago. And so would everyone else. So how about assisting me, folks? Have I stumbled across a little romance? Are we going to hear wedding bells?" She smiled eagerly, arranging her pad and pencil to jot down a few notes.

"We're just friends," Patrick repeated. "Miss Waring and I are going back to the dance now, Jane. Can I get you a drink before we go?"

Jane stood up, too. "I can't write here. I'll go into the coffee shop to make my notes. So there's really nothing between you two?" she asked, and pinned them with a pair of bright, intelligent eyes.

"As I said, just friends."

Jane scowled. "Don't you ever do anything but *work*, Barron? All work and no play makes for a damned dull story. Nice to have met you, Ms. Waring."

She turned and strode briskly from the bar. "Sorry about that," Patrick said. "You can't be rude to them, especially at a time like this. As Jane mentioned, she's doing a feature on me."

"I understand," Elinor said. She felt a small glow of satisfaction to know that Patrick spent most of his time at work.

"Why don't we go somewhere more...private," he suggested.

Elinor hesitated a moment. She looked hard at Patrick. I'm probably being a Grade A idiot, she thought, but said it anyway. "Want to come over to my place?"

He reached for her hand. "I thought you'd never ask."

Chapter Three

Patrick looked at the van and smiled. "The Plant Shed," he read aloud. "A modest name. Does it have special significance?"

"It sure does. I started small. I've grown out of the shed now, but I kept the name."

"It figures you'd be interested in your roots."

Even this seemingly innocent subject brought Elinor memories of the past. In hindsight she realized that although a lack of money was one of the major reasons they hadn't married, it hadn't really taken all that much money to start her business. She could also have started that small in Washington.

"Better wipe off the seat," she said. "I had a very special passenger sitting there today. I had to belt it in."

"Animal, vegetable or mineral?" he said, wiping a light coating of earth from the leather seat.

She smiled at him. "If I say 'very special,' you don't have to ask. It was a plant—a big beautiful hibiscus in full bloom. I wish I could have kept it."

"I bet that's the hardest part of the job, parting with your friends."

"Yes, and the second hardest part is *not* parting with them. I feel sorry for the ones not chosen," she explained. "The wallflowers that nobody wants."

"Except you."

They drove the short distance to her apartment through newly fallen snow. Halos of blue and yellow gleamed from the street lamps. The Maple Drive apartment complex where Elinor lived was a group of six buildings, each holding twelve apartments, four to a floor. What had attracted her to this modest place, other than the low rent, was the resemblance to a small village. The buildings were clustered around an open square that was landscaped with trees and flowers when it was warmer. In winter, the square looked desolate, with dark limbs clawing the sky and shrubs hunching under their blanket of snow.

"It's pretty in summer," she said. "The kids play in the square, and the older residents feed the squirrels and tend the flowers. Kind of homey."

He nodded. "I'll bet you lead the gardening brigade."

She laughed. "I must admit I weed a few beds."

She parked in the garage behind her building and they went to her apartment. "We don't have an elevator, and I'm on the third floor. I hope your legs are strong," she said.

"If they're not, they should be. I have a long race ahead of me." Patrick mentally noted that her business couldn't be that profitable if she didn't have a private car and lived in a walk-up apartment. Of course, she was obviously happy, and that was the main thing.

Once inside, he saw that she had created her own special brand of magic. Patrick had thought it would be like this—a tropical garden. Her old rooms in New York had possessed the same ambience. It wasn't just the spruce tree in the corner that glimmered with bulbs and tinsel. It wasn't the small forest of plants in front of the window and balcony door and hanging helter-skelter from hooks in the ceiling. It was the very air itself, warm and soft and scented with the quiet perfume of growing things. He knew she kept it humidified, for the sake of her plants. There was an aura of peace and well-being here.

He glanced around at the rest of the place. It was utilitarian but pretty, with a tweedy sort of sofa, a leather padded chair, a wall of shelves holding books, a stereo and a TV. The paintings, including a series of sketches of flowers, were all plant related.

"Just make yourself at home," Elinor said. "I'll be right back."

"I feel at home already," he smiled, gazing around at the various plants. "Do you still have Adam and Eve?" he asked.

She had forgotten his nickname for the pair of jade plants, grown into trees now, from which sprang such a plethora of young jades. "They're in my conservatory at my parents' home. They're too big for this little place. Of course, I maintain visiting rights."

"And adoption rights to all the offspring, I see," he teased, looking at the pots in front of her window. They, too, had grown to a respectable size now.

"Of course. I have their elder offspring here," she said, looking at the jades. "The little plants sell for over a dollar each. And you remember how prolific Adam and Eve are."

She ducked into her bedroom but didn't intend to change out of her dress. Its very formality gave her a feeling of protection and she knew she needed protection from the temptation in the next room. She just wanted to tidy her hair and freshen her lipstick.

When she returned, Patrick was standing at the window, becoming acquainted with her plants. It seemed so right for him to be here yet the black evening suit reminded her of the time that had passed since their relationship ended. It was no rented suit. It fit him like a glove, clinging to his broad shoulders and lean body. He moved in loftier circles now. He walked toward her and lamplight caught his hair.

"I've been having a word with them," he said. "I expect you still chat to your plants?"

"People at the store started giving me funny looks, so we have silent conversations now. It's really just the attention they crave."

His dark eyes turned to hers and held for a distracting moment. "Don't we all?"

"Why don't I turn on the Christmas tree lights?" she said, tripping over the mound of presents in the process. "As you can see, I've got my Christmas shopping and wrapping all done. I'll be taking these to the farm." Why am I babbling like an incoherent idiot? she silently wondered.

"You'll have the van full." Patrick stood by the sofa, waiting for her to sit down.

She again felt that reluctance mixed with anticipation. "Would you like something to drink? Coffee, tea?"

"Herbal? That maté tea you used to serve was nice. It was almost a sleeping draft. Do you still make it?"

"I think I have a can somewhere. Want something to eat?" What am I saying? I don't have any snack food on hand!

"No, thanks."

Patrick followed her to the kitchen. She wished she'd asked him to put on some tapes, to keep him in the other room. The kitchen was so small he hovered at the doorway while she prepared the tea, overpowering her senses. The ambivalence of familiarity and strangeness was even stronger here, and his formal wear looked out of place in her modest apartment.

He must have watched her make maté a hundred times, yet she felt he was observing her as if it were the first time. It made her self-conscious. She felt clumsy. The tea canister rattled noisily, and when she poured the water, it sloshed into the saucer. She wiped it up and handed him his own cup to take into the living room, in case she spilled it.

They sat companionably on the sofa, with the tea on the table in front of them. "Your apartment's very homey, Ellie. I always picture you like this."

His words held interesting undertones. They showed that he gave her more than a passing thought, at least. "Tell me all about your work," she urged. She was interested in it, but his talking also gave her time to collect her wits.

He talked about the civil rights organization, his initial eagerness and his eventual realization that it took more to get the job done. She led him to tell her about his present work and future plans. "Do you think you'd like being a congressman?" she asked.

"I'd like having some influence to do what I want to do. Politics is where the power lies. The rest of it, the PR and hand pumping and kowtowing to the press, goes with the territory. I hope you weren't put off by Jane Eliot. It's her job, and she's good at it."

"What kind of an article is she doing?"

"It's a major story, background as well as my present work. Firth tells me my profile isn't high enough, so this is a real coup for me. The *Journal*'s an influential paper. It could be a big help to me in getting the party nomination. Jane feels the personal side of it is a little skimpy. Probably because my private life *is* rather thin," he added ruefully. "I don't have a lot of time to spend with friends. I miss that, of course."

Patrick sighed and smiled at her rather sadly. It was so pleasant being with Ellie again, just talking, not worrying about every word he said.

"Apparently that other guy, Tony Gower, spends too much time with friends," she mentioned.

"People of the female persuasion. They can hardly be called friends."

"He's quite a womanizer, I take it?"

"Well, just between us, that's why Firth decided he has to go. Politicians have to be like Caesar's wife, not only innocent but above suspicion." He smiled at her. "And if this is giving you the idea that I'm as squeaky clean as Calpurnia, I don't mind a bit. There hasn't been anyone since—" He came to a stop and found himself drowning in her stormy eyes. "Since you, Ellie. No one serious, I mean." Would there ever be another Elinor Waring in his life? he mused. Had he made a terrible mistake to give her up?

His hand reached for hers and squeezed it. Elinor gazed into his eyes and felt almost hypnotized. They were a deep, navy blue, with tiny flecks of gold. She saw regret and a question in them.

"You said you aren't seeing anyone, either."

"My work has kept me pretty busy, too."

"Do you think—did we do the right thing, all those years ago?"

The breath swelled in her lungs until it seemed she'd suffocate. A part of her had wanted to hear something like this, yet the problems that went with the question were nearly overwhelming. While these scattered thoughts scuttled through her mind, she noted that Patrick had moved closer to her.

"I don't know, Patrick. I wonder sometimes." Her voice was unsteady, and when his hand brushed her cheek, she fell silent, unable to go on. His hand lingered a moment, while the hushed air around them seemed to listen.

Later, she didn't know which of them had actually begun the kiss. It just happened, because of that irrevocable attraction, they acted like magnets drawing together. His lips seemed to come closer, but maybe she was the one leaning toward him. She only knew that when his lips found hers, it was like coming home after a long, lonesome journey. And the arrival was one of heady excitement. The first tentative touching set off shock waves of longing that stirred her to the core of being.

His arms were around her, crushing her against him, while his lips bruised hers in a searing kiss. She had to touch him with her hands, renewing familiarity. Her fingers stroked the smooth crispness of his hair, before sliding down his neck, then to the broad flare of shoulder muscles. She reveled in his strength, the male feel of him. It had been so long. The vague thought drifted through her mind that she was fortunate above other women, to have not only a devastatingly handsome man in love with her but one of unblemished character.

His lips moved hungrily, and all such thoughts left her mind. She was aware only of the unspoken need she sensed in his embrace and the answering need that washed through her in a wave. She knew now that there hadn't been any other women for him, nor any other man for her. It had always been Patrick, all the years she tried to tell herself their parting had been for the best. *This* was the best, being with him, loving him, feeling his love for her. She felt her heart thud against him and wondered if he felt its betraying rhythm, too.

He pulled back and buried his face in the curve of her chin, nibbling her throat with engrossing kisses, just where the pulse beat. "The feeling's still there, isn't it, darling? It just doesn't go away," he murmured softly. She sensed an air of bewilderment in his question.

"Are you sure we want it to? Go away, I mean?" she asked, and realized the same sound of bewilderment in her own words. This was crazy. They were both rational people. They had to take charge.

He didn't answer but just looked at her silently a moment. When he spoke, it was a strange answer. "I wonder if we have anything to say about it."

It sounded as if he felt this same helpless, overpowering attraction. "Oh, Patrick, it's all so difficult!" She sighed.

He tilted her chin up and smiled into her moist eyes. "The things that are worth having are usually difficult but worth fighting for. It'll work out somehow in the end. You'll see."

Buoyed by his confidence, she agreed. "We'll work it out, somehow."

Patrick realized he had let the situation get out of hand. He should never have kissed her. Now his words were being twisted, and he sensed danger. "It'll work out" wasn't the same as "we'll work it out," yet her answer had thrilled him. He hadn't come here to stir up the past, but to pave the road for his political career. It didn't matter if Ellie was still bothersomely appealing. This definitely wasn't the time to resume that affair. He must stop, now!

He pulled away from Elinor and sat up, straightening his tie. "Of course, I'll be very busy in the immediate future," he said, trying for an air of ease. He was still nervous, and without the proper softening frills, he said, "I nearly forgot why I called you! Your charms distracted me."

She looked at him, curious. "What is it? You mentioned I might be able to help."

"I hope you can. You remember those letters we exchanged that first summer you spent at your folks' farm?"

"Yes, of course." She frowned in perplexity, wondering what they could possibly have to do with the present situation.

"I don't suppose you kept them?" The mood had changed dramatically. He wore a guarded look now.

"Why do you ask?"

Damn, I'm making a mess of this, Patrick thought as he ran his fingers through his thick hair. "As I recall, they weren't exactly discreet," he said.

"We had just fallen in love that spring."

"And I missed you so much I didn't think I'd last the summer without you. If they landed in the wrong hands..."

"There was nothing wrong with them," she replied.

"They're not treasonous, but they're pretty indiscreet. You remember what I said about Caesar's wife? A candidate for political office has to be not only innocent but above suspicion. Everyone's especially sensitive to that sort of thing recently, and I did more than pour out my heart. As I recall, that was the summer I discovered Plato's *Republic*. I may have unwisely quoted a few admiring phrases on communism. Plato's communism has nothing to do with the totalitarianism of today, but my words could be twisted.

I'd feel a lot safer if I could get those letters back and burn them."

Burn them! He wanted to burn her love letters! Letters that she had tied up in a pink ribbon and kept in the bottom drawer of her dresser. Even worse, that was why he had called her tonight. He didn't want to marry her. He didn't even want to *see* her. He just wanted his letters back. Like an idiot, she had been willing to fall into his arms. He was using love as a weapon to get his own way. Her spine stiffened, and when she spoke, her voice held an edge of sarcasm. "What makes you think I kept them?"

"Then you got rid of them," he said, leaping to the wrong conclusion.

Elinor didn't correct him. Pride kept her from telling the truth, that she'd treasured them over the years, unwilling to sever her last link to Patrick. She was also curious to hear what he'd say next.

"Firth had a long talk with me when he asked me if I was interested in running," he explained. "He quizzed me all about my past—the usual things that come up to smear a candidate. Cheating on exams, drugs, criminal record, sex."

"I thought we were talking about love."

"You know what I mean. They go together, although you *can* have one without the other."

"Cheating and drugs and crime... Funny, I wouldn't have included love in that list myself."

"You're right, of course. Love belongs in a list with moonbeams and orchids...and Elinor Waring."

His smile seemed lovingly intimate and sincere. If she hadn't known him so well, she would have been fooled. She decided to push him farther and bring the situation to a head. "What we were talking about a moment ago, Patrick—how are we going to work this thing out, you in Washington and me here?"

He thought for a moment before answering. It would be nice to see Ellie again. Damned hard to arrange, but nice. Maybe this time they were mature enough to work it out. "We'll have to keep it on the back burner for a while, I'm afraid. I'll be campaigning my socks off, but I'll make a point to come to Delta as often as I can, and I hope you'll visit me in Washington. I'd really like to see you, Ellie."

Elinor took a deep breath. She felt as if she were swallowing poison. So she was to be kept on the back burner. "But after you're elected, you'll be even busier," she pointed out.

A smile peeped down at her. "I sure could use a wife," he said, and kissed the corner of her jaw.

"So your friend Jane Eliot mentioned." But he had gotten Jane off that track in a hurry. Now Elinor knew he had no intention of marrying her. She realized that he'd say whatever he had to say to make a graceful exit, once they'd arranged this meeting for him to get back his letters.

Her chest felt heavy with regrets and disappointment, but she'd be damned if she'd let him see how much she hurt. She stood and said in as calm a voice as she could muster, "You probably have an early morning planned, like me. Among other things, I have to deliver to the hotel a hundred and fifty of those poinsettias I mentioned. So, shall we call it a night?"

Patrick rose, too, reluctantly. "I guess we better. Firth wants a meeting before we hit the sack. I'll call you tomorrow, okay? I'm booked for lunch and dinner, but at four o'clock I have half an hour."

"A whole half hour!"

"I'm sorry, but you see how it is. I promise to clear up everything and we'll have one whole evening together before I leave. You don't know how I'm looking forward to it."

He didn't even ask whether *she* had an evening free, or which evening would be convenient for her. "I'm booked up pretty tight, too," she mentioned.

His eyebrows rose. "I thought you weren't seeing anyone!"

"No one special, I said. I also don't sit at home every night talking to my plants."

"Of course not. That was thoughtless of me. I just thought maybe you could rearrange your schedule, since no one special is involved."

"Yes, I know what you thought, Patrick."

"I'll talk to Firth tonight and call you tomorrow at four. You'll be at your shop?"

"Yes." And he arrogantly assumed she could leave it.

"Good. I'll call you there and we'll arrange something. I've got to go now. Good night, Ellie. It was wonderful seeing you again." He gave her a quick kiss on the lips and left.

"Get out while the getting's good" was the phrase that popped into his mind as he hurried downstairs and out into the cold air. There wasn't a taxi in sight. In his haste he hadn't thought to call a cab, and he found himself in an unknown part of town, wandering around, looking for the main street. He shouldn't have promised Ellie he'd call her tomorrow. She didn't have the letters, so he didn't have to see her again. He thought about calling and making an excuse. But when he looked all around at the ghostlike banks of snow, he smiled. In his heart he knew he'd call. In truth, he could hardly wait till the next afternoon.

Elinor was so angry she couldn't keep still. She stormed around her apartment, muttering to herself. "That egotist! He thinks he can come storming back into my life and I'll rearrange it to suit him. He thinks he's so perfect, with his squeaky clean reputation." So he thought love was a crime, like drugs and cheating. Well, he didn't know the first thing about love. All he knew was politics and chumming up to the press. She'd been wrong to think he hadn't changed. He had changed—completely, utterly—from the Patrick Barron she used to know. He had become a politician.

And that political animal was very concerned about those scorching love letters he'd written to her when he was still a mere human mortal. Elinor hadn't looked at them for a year, but she got them out that night and read them through, skimming over the recital of his activities to closely read the more intimate parts. They had been going together for only two months when the college term was over, and she had gone home for the summer. Pat had stayed in New York and written her at least three times a week, sometimes every day. They were passionate love letters that had thrilled her then as much as they grieved her now, knowing the writer had changed.

What was he so worried about, anyway? she wondered. Did he actually think she'd show her private, intimate correspondence to the press, for heaven's sake? She'd never do anything like that, but she wouldn't burn them, either.

After she had read them, however, she decided maybe she should give them back or burn them. What was the point of keeping written promises after the love had died? She *would* burn them. She even got out some matches and wondered where she could safely perform that awful deed, since she didn't have a fireplace.

But Elinor didn't really want to burn those letters. Since she didn't like having even intimated a lie to Patrick, she decided she'd say she had found them in a drawer, which wasn't a lie. She *had* found them; they just hadn't been lost. She'd give them back. Then he'd never have to worry about them again. He could forget them and her. But first they'd have just one more meeting. It didn't occur to her that there was more than one way of playing with fire.

She tied the pile back up in their pink ribbon, then took it off and replaced the ribbon with an elastic band, so he wouldn't get the idea she had any sentimental interest in them. Pink satin ribbon was too revealing.

In a sad, nostalgic mood, she went to commune with her plants. Her fingers lightly stroked the fronds of the Madagascar dragon tree. With its somber color and drooping leaves, it seemed to match her mood. "It wouldn't have worked out anyway," she said. "I don't want to leave Delta. I'm happy here. I love my nursery and my shop. What do I want with a politician? I won't even vote for him. Damned if I will."

This spirit of rebellion made her feel better, though she didn't really fool herself. She'd vote for Patrick. She'd miss him, too. She wouldn't miss the new Patrick who came in his black jacket and white tie. No, she'd miss the old Patrick, who used to walk through the snow with her, laughing. They hadn't laughed much tonight.

It was difficult for Elinor to sleep, but about one o'clock she finally dozed off and slept soundly.

In the morning, the letters on Elinor's desk at home reminded her she'd be hearing from Pat at four. He obviously didn't care too much about seeing her, because even if he showed up at the shop promptly, he couldn't stay for more than fifteen minutes before he'd have to leave again. She thought about sending the letters to him but decided they'd be safer at home. If he wanted them, he'd have to come and get them.

At work, there wasn't time to think of Patrick. It was infernally busy, with Christmas drawing near. Elinor always enjoyed this time of year. Everyone was in such a good mood. "Merry Christmas" seemed to resound from every corner. And the reassuring tinkle of the cash register felt good, too.

She had bought small potted evergreen seedlings and decorated them herself. Dozens of festooned Christmas trees only two feet high twinkled from shelves and countertops, with the showier display of poinsettias lording it over lesser flowers. They came in many colors now, such as white and various shades of pink, but the familiar bright red was still her favorite.

Poinsettias were selling faster than peanuts at a ball game. In the morning, she helped her clerk, Clare Evans, in the shop. That afternoon she had to take a van load of poinsettias to the hotel. She'd be back at the shop by four for Pat's call.

Elinor knew Patrick was very busy, but she also knew that Firth's group was staying at the Delta Arms Hotel, and she wondered if she'd see him. The flowers were distributed over many parts of the large building: the lobby, the formal dining room, the coffee shop. She peered around for a sight of him as she moved from place to place. The hotel was swarming with people, but she didn't see any politician she recognized. The last dozen plants were destined for the coffee shop. She brought them in on a wheeled dolly, which was hard to drag over the carpets.

As she arranged the last plants, she saw Congressman Firth enter the coffee shop. He was accompanied by half a dozen flunkies, as befitted a congressman. Patrick was, symbolically, at his right hand.

Elinor's heart gave a painful lurch at the sight of him. Whatever Patrick's faults, he was the most handsome man she'd ever dated. He looked up, saw her and stopped dead in his tracks. He smiled. Just a very small smile, but she could see his eyes glow with pleasure.

His sudden halt threw the little group into a moment's confusion. Firth turned to speak to Patrick, who suddenly wasn't there. He was a step behind, apologizing to Tony Gower, who had bumped into him from behind.

"That's the lady you were with last night, isn't it?" Tony asked. He ran a quick, assessing look over Elinor.

"Yes," Patrick replied.

"What's her name?"

Firth turned and asked Patrick a question, which saved him from having to either answer Tony or be rude to him. As the group went to a table, Patrick gave himself a silent lecture. *Wake up, Barron. Business and pleasure don't mix, remember?* But that fleeting glimpse of Ellie had startled him. For a moment, he felt that it was three years ago, and he was back in New York. Ellie looked so much like her old self, with her tousled head peering out from behind two flourishing plants, like Mother Nature's own daughter.

The group settled into a corner table and ordered coffee. While they waited for it to arrive, Pat excused himself and went to have a word with Elinor.

She had just finished her work and was wiping earth and a few bits of dried leaf from her jacket. Her face was rosy from the exercise of hauling and lifting all those plants.

Patrick came up quietly from behind to surprise her. "Fancy meeting you here," he said, and pulled her behind a spreading palm for a moment's privacy.

"Patrick!"

"In the flesh," he said, smiling. He held on to her hand while they talked. "You look as if you've been chopping trees. Your work must be harder than I thought."

And he looked perfect. Every hair was in place, his jacket unwrinkled, his shirt crisp. As his blue eyes examined her, Elinor felt a stab of annoyance that he was seeing her so disheveled. "Your work must be easier," she snapped. "You don't look as if you've been exerting yourself."

"Au contraire," he said playfully. "I have consumed six cups of coffee, read three reports, attended umpteen meetings, shaken umpteen dozen hands and I have a TV interview scheduled for four o'clock—a *network* interview," he added importantly. "Not just a local affair. The country will be seeing me in its living room at six-thirty, standard time."

Elinor noticed that he'd forgotten his promise to phone her at four. She could hardly hope to compete with the networks, but her annoyance congealed to anger all the same. "Then it's lucky we happened to meet."

"I've been calling you ever since the interview was arranged. I wanted to give you the opportunity to admire me on TV," he added playfully.

"I certainly wouldn't want to miss that—especially since it seems I'm going to be deprived of my half hour."

"Not deprived, just delayed. I've rescheduled it for ten-thirty, if you're free?" He looked eagerly for her reaction.

"I'll make it a point to be free. I have something important to tell you."

His voice lowered to an intimate whisper, and his eyes glowed. "That sounds promising."

His tone, a sort of teasing croon, hinted at romance. Elinor schooled her own voice to pure business and said matter-of-factly, "On second thought, maybe you'd better hear my news now. I found your letters, the ones you wrote to me a few years ago."

"I thought you'd gotten rid of them."

"Well, after you left, I half remembered seeing them with some other papers I keep in a drawer. You know—diplomas, receipts, warranties. I checked, and sure enough, there they were." She spoke in a jaunty voice, as though the letters had no more importance to her than the other paper detritus of her past.

But Patrick looked pleased with her news. "You kept them!" He smiled. "I've still got yours, too, bundled up in silver paper."

"We'll exchange then."

"Are you running for an elected position, too?" he joked.

"You never know. Look, since they're so important to you, I could send them to the hotel if—"

"No! I don't want them floating around the hotel."

"I could burn them," she suggested.

"Before you do, I'd like to read them again. Why don't you leave them at your place? I'll meet you there at ten-thirty and we'll have a bonfire."

"All right. You'd better bring a fireplace. I don't have one. I'll let you get back to your group now. I have to go myself." She turned to leave.

"Wait!" He grasped her arm. "I'm sorry about having to break our first date. I tried to get in touch with you. I wish we had more time together."

She smiled brightly, though her heart was heavy. "We'll just have to make the most of what we have."

"That's the spirit! At least we'll have the rest of the evening."

"It won't take that long to burn a couple of dozen letters," she said, and walked away, the dignity of her exit hampered by having to drag the plant dolly after her.

Patrick stood with his head cocked to one side, watching her departure. Ellie did wonderful things to a pair of tightly fitting jeans.

Tony Gower peered his head around the corner and grinned. "Sorry to interrupt, but the big boy wants you, Pat."

"Yes, coming. I'll be right there."

"Who's your friend?"

"Just a woman I knew at college," Patrick replied, and quickly changed the subject. "What does Firth want? Did he say?"

Tony gave a sharp look, and Patrick was glad when the other man dropped the subject.

He never guessed that Tony was wondering if there was something Patrick wanted to hide about Elinor.

Chapter Four

Elinor stared at the empty desk, rubbed her eyes and stared again. It was impossible. It was just plain impossible. She'd left the letters on her desk, held together with a brown elastic band. They'd been there when she went to work that morning, but they were gone now, when she came home after work.

Maybe she hadn't left them on her desk! She made a mad dash around the apartment. She knew she hadn't put them in the kitchen, but she looked there anyway. They weren't on the table, or on the counter, or in any of the utensil drawers. The letters weren't in her bedroom, where they could have fallen under the dresser or been accidentally knocked into a drawer. She even looked in the bathroom. When all the possible places had been searched, she began looking in spots where no sane person would ever put a pile of letters. They weren't in the cupboards or in the cookie jar. When she found herself looking in the fridge, she pulled herself back to her senses.

All right, Elinor, accept the truth, she told herself. They were gone. Who could have taken them? The first thing that occurred to her was that Patrick had already picked them up by having gotten the janitor to let him into her apartment. He didn't want her to send them to the hotel, and maybe he was uneasy with the idea of their being left in the apartment unattended. Who else would want them?

Before long, it occurred to her that Patrick might have picked up the letters because something had come up and he wasn't going to be able to see her that evening. She felt a heavy, sagging disappointment. After she spent a moment pacing, an even worse idea popped into her head, an idea that turned her disappointment to anger. He didn't want to see her. He'd taken the letters so he wouldn't *have* to see her. Anger scalded her throat, but after she'd calmed down, Elinor realized she should just check with the janitor.

He wasn't in, of course. One of the mysteries of life at Maple Drive was where the janitor spent his time.

Maybe she should call Patrick. She called the hotel, but he wasn't in his room. The operator had no idea where he was but said there was a formal dinner at seven-thirty in the dining room with the congressman and the local party organizers. She could have Mr. Barron paged there.

It didn't seem like a good idea to interrupt him at an important dinner. "No, I'll try again later," Elinor said. If dinner was at seven-thirty, he might be in his room to change at seven. She phoned back at seven.

He still didn't answer, so she left a message for him to call.

"I believe Mr. Barron has already been to his room to change," the operator said in a confidential voice. "I happened to see him and Congressman Firth hurry through the lobby to a limousine. They were already dressed for evening. Some political business before the dinner, I expect."

Elinor sighed. She asked to have him call her when and if the friendly operator spotted him. When he hadn't called by eight, she assumed he had gotten into the dining room unseen by the operator. There was nothing to do but wait. At eight-fifteen, Gillie Parson dropped in to say hello.

"Wow, the station is in pandemonium this week," she said as she flopped onto the sofa and kicked off her slippers. "We've been taping interviews all day."

"It's unusual for Delta to have so many celebrities in town," Elinor said.

"Yeah, between the bankers and the politicians, it's like Grand Central Station at WHYM. Luke says they're already gearing up for the elections next November. Both parties will be running new representatives, so they're trying to get publicity. Luke was surprised Tony Gower wasn't there, but guess what, Ellie. It seems the Democrats might be running your friend Pat Barron!"

"Yes, I heard about it."

"Oh." Gillie sounded disappointed. "Well, anyway, the Republicans had Harry Thornby there, of course, the guy who used to be the mayor of Corning. I went down to the hotel to meet Luke last night and

met Thornby. One of his aides came back to my place
with Luke and me for coffee. Rosco something, his
name was. He was really interesting. His wife's in one
of the afternoon soaps, but she wasn't with him.''

Elinor was only half listening. She kept thinking
about the letters. "You didn't happen to see anyone
around my apartment today, did you, Gillie?'' Sometimes Gillie didn't go to work till ten and came home
at irregular hours.

"No, why? You weren't burgled, were you?'' she
demanded, jumping to attention.

"No—well, maybe.'' She told Gillie about the situation.

"You mean you were out with Pat Barron and
didn't tell me!'' she exclaimed. "Ellie, that's terrific!
You know a guy who might be in Congress. Too bad
you broke up with him. Do you think there's any
chance of getting back together?'' she asked eagerly.

"Don't be silly. He only called me because of the
letters, and now I can't find them.''

"Why don't you call the janitor?''

"I did, but I'll try him again.'' Elinor phoned again.
He was in this time, but he hadn't let anyone into her
apartment. He hadn't seen anyone suspicious hanging around but his own rooms were in another building.

"I'm going to get another chain on my door,'' Gillie said.

"Chains aren't much good once you leave. The
locks on these doors are a disgrace. I'm going to get a
dead bolt installed, at my own expense if necessary.
Anyone can get into the building. We don't even have

an intercom to tell us who's ringing our bell. All they'd have to do is ring half a dozen apartments, and someone would push the button to open the front door."

"Yeah, Luke says I should move. Now, if he could only convince the station to give me a raise. So how's my fern doing?"

"Drying out. It takes longer than a day to recover from massive drowning."

Gillie soon left, and Elinor kept fretting over the letters. She was half-convinced Patrick had somehow managed to get them without the janitor's help. If he didn't call at ten-thirty, she'd assume he had already got them and that was the only reason he'd bothered making that date.

She was in a bad mood as she prepared her dinner, and she tried to work herself out of it by a little self-pampering. She grilled a steak and made a Caesar salad. She ate in front of the Christmas tree, with the lights on and some Christmas hymns playing on the tape deck. It didn't help. After she had cleaned up the kitchen, she finally got around to watching a videotape on orchids. They were beautiful but too much work for her to try raising them at this time.

At ten o'clock, Elinor decided to change out of her work clothes, just in case Patrick actually decided to honor her with a flying visit. She could hardly wear spotted jeans when he'd be in formal evening wear, but she wouldn't get all dressed up, either. Just a skirt and blouse, not even her new blouse but last year's scarlet silk. Her dark hair and eyes could meet the demands of scarlet, and its strong brilliance always lifted her spirits. She dallied with her preparations, half keeping an eye on the clock. She couldn't find anything else to add to either her face or blouse and decided to look at the Christmas tree to wait.

She'd always had mixed emotions about killing a beautiful tree that had taken years to grow, just for a few weeks' viewing. But Christmas wouldn't be Christmas without that resinous scent filling the air. Plastic trees were too perfect. Besides, the trees were a cash crop for some farmers, and a renewable resource.

She thought again about the letters. Worrying made her nervous, and she decided to let a cup of maté tea settle her nerves. Before the kettle had come to the boil, her buzzer sounded and she dashed to answer it. Could it actually be Patrick, and on time? No, she must be imagining things. It was probably Clare, her shop assistant. She lived in one of the Maple Drive apartments, too, and often stopped by. It flashed through her mind that maybe Pat really did want to see her.

In thirty seconds she was peering through the peephole in her door and saw Patrick. He was shrunk to a smaller size and slightly deformed by the peephole, but it was undeniably him. He was wearing another evening suit. This new life seemed to require a lot of formality.

She opened the door and felt a smile grow unbidden at the sight of him. "I see you're formal again. Do you live in this outfit?"

"Only after six. I have three. A pair and a spare, in case of accidents. I'm getting used to it."

Buying one evening dress had seemed like an extravagance to her. "Well, you're on time!" she said, trying not to sound impressed, and he walked in.

"You seem surprised! Wasn't I always on time, more or less? I keep a tighter schedule now. Punctuality is even more important."

"I suppose that means you have to leave in two minutes?"

"I've arranged this evening for us," he announced, and pulled her into his arms for a welcoming kiss. His face felt cold against hers. His overcoat was cold, too, yet the overall feeling was one of warmth, rising to heat as his lips clung. "Let's not waste a minute of it," he murmured in her ear, while his arms pulled her closer.

They went hand in hand into the living room. The visit had begun so well that Elinor was sorry she had to risk the mood by mentioning the letters, but it was too important to put off. "Patrick, about the letters—you *did* pick them up this afternoon, I hope?"

He looked perfectly bewildered. "How could I? I don't have a key to your place. You're not telling me..." They had just sat down. He rose abruptly and stared down at her in confusion. "Ellie!"

She swallowed and said in a very small voice, "They're gone."

His hand gripped his forehead and for a moment his face clenched like a fist. When he spoke, his voice was hard. "Dammit! Are you sure?"

"Positive. They're gone."

"When?"

"I noticed it when I got home, a little after six."

"Six! But that was *hours* ago! Why didn't you call me?" His voice was tinged with anger, and his inky eyes held an accusation. "You knew how important they were to me."

Her voice rose in angry defense. "I *did* call you! I've been calling the hotel, leaving messages, ever since I found out. If you ever stayed in one place for two minutes—"

Patrick put a calming hand on her shoulder. "I'm sorry. I didn't mean to blow up at you. It's not your fault, but this could be serious. You're sure they've been taken? You didn't put them back in that dark corner?"

"They were right on that desk," she said, pointing to it.

Patrick hurried to the desk and moved a few bills and letters around.

"I looked everywhere, through all the drawers," she added when he began pulling them open to search. "I've searched the whole apartment, Patrick. They're not here. I'm sorry. Someone must have broken in and taken them. Who do you think would have done it?"

"Presumably the opposition, Harry Thornby's crew. Those letters will give them some good ammunition in the election."

"The letters aren't that bad," she said, trying to console him. "It's not as if you were a married man or something. They're letters from a bachelor to a girl-friend, and they're three years old. You were young then."

"They're terrible," he groaned, sinking his head in his hand. Elinor felt a wince of pain that he was ashamed of his love for her. "How did anyone get in here? Was the lock busted?" he demanded.

"No, I had no idea anyone had been here till I saw the letters were missing," she replied stiffly. "I've already called the janitor. He didn't let in anyone claiming to be a relative or friend. My neighbor didn't see anyone, either."

"They wouldn't do it when they had an audience," he said rather grimly. He went to the door and examined the lock. "A child could break in here. Especially since the TV detective shows have given lessons on how to use a credit card to do it. You should get a better lock for your own protection."

"Yes. Well, what do you plan to do about the letters?"

Patrick stared into the distance, his mind apparently miles away. "Get them back. There's plenty of time. Rosco won't use them till the election race. They have nothing against my running, so they won't use them yet."

The name rang a bell. "Rosco! That's it!" she exclaimed.

He looked at her, surprised. "How do you know Thornby's henchman?"

"Patrick, he was at my neighbor's house last night. You don't suppose—no, the letters were still here this morning."

He sounded excited at the news. "He was here? What time?"

"I'm not sure. Fairly early, I think. My neighbor, Gillie, mentioned something about those interviews at the chamber of commerce dinner. Her boyfriend did the interviews. She met some of Thornby's crew, and Rosco came back here after. I remember the name distinctly."

"He might have seen us arrive," Patrick said, frowning. "We didn't stay out very late ourselves. He'd be interested enough to check up on my friends."

"Is there anything I can do to help you?"

"You can ask your friend if she mentioned your name."

Elinor jumped up. "I'll call her right now." But when she dialed, there was no answer. "She'll probably be out all evening."

"Too bad. I can't wait till morning. Harry Thornby's group is staying at the Delta Arms Hotel, where we've all been put up. I imagine the letters are in one of their rooms by now. Not Harry's. He wouldn't be directly involved. It'd be Rosco who has them. There's no way of retrieving them—unless..." He paused and frowned.

Elinor looked surprised. "You mean..."

"Yes, stealing them back. Don't look like that, Ellie. It's not as though I were stealing candy from a baby. In fact, it isn't stealing at all. It's recovering stolen property. They're *your* letters. It's beginning to sound like a duty to me," he added, peering to see if he had convinced her. When the look of opposition had faded from her features, he said, "I have to get into Rosco's room."

Once Elinor was convinced, she wished she could help. "Maybe I can do something along that line," she said uncertainly. "I know a lot of the personnel there, from doing the flowers every week."

Patrick flashed her a quick look. "I don't want you to risk your job, Ellie. The manager wouldn't like it if he found you breaking and entering guests' rooms."

"Let's hope he doesn't catch us then," she said, and ran for her coat. Her ability to help made her heart feel little lighter. Besides, just being with Patrick had always been fun. It wasn't the way she had envisaged their evening together, but she felt guilty about deceiving Patrick about those letters. If she'd just given them back right away, none of this would have happened.

When they went downstairs, Elinor was surprised to see a long, sleek, black, chauffeur-driven limousine parked in front of the building. She ignored it, and headed toward the garage. Patrick took her arm and stopped her. "We're traveling in style tonight. Mr. Firth lent me the wheels. I had planned a romantic extravaganza, beginning with champagne in the back seat, with dinner to follow."

"Dinner in the car?"

"Dinner in Delta's finest restaurant, the evening culminating in—well, it was a nice dream anyway." He gave a rueful smile. She wondered what culmination he had planned for the evening.

The chauffeur, a broad-shouldered hulk of a man, hopped out and held the door for them. "Back to the hotel, Ron," Patrick said.

A window behind the front seat gave them privacy once they were seated on the luxurious, plush seats. "You men really travel in style," she exclaimed, impressed in spite of herself.

"We work hard, and we play hard. But business before pleasure. We have one bit of good luck and one bad. The good luck is that the Republicans are tied up at a planning session tonight."

"And the bad?"

"The session is taking place at the hotel. Rosco might just decide to leave and take a run up to his room. They're all on the seventh floor. Can you find out which room is Rosco's?"

"Depends who's on the desk."

"Let's cross our fingers, then," he suggested, and immediately made crossing their fingers impossible by holding her hand. "It's too bad. I was really looking forward to tonight." He sounded sad.

"We might get lucky and find the letters right away."

"Hold that thought."

The limousine ride was so smooth it was like sitting on a comfortable sofa in the living room. The white snowbanks along sidewalks spoke of icy temperatures, but inside it was as warm as summer. As they entered the main street, the multicolored Christmas lights and bright store windows created a fairyland atmosphere. The sidewalks were nearly empty at this hour, with all the stores closed.

They made their plans as the car, expertly managed by the chauffeur, sped through traffic. "The tricky part is going to be getting hold of a key for the room," Patrick said. "I've already been making myself known, and if I've done a good job, the staff will know I'm not with Thornby's party. Have you got any ideas?"

"I think our best bet is for me to try to get hold of a master key from the cleaning crew. Stop the car, Pat."

He looked across the seat and smiled. "This is the first time you've called me Pat."

"Sorry, I forgot you like the full dignity of Patrick. I never objected to your calling me Ellie."

"That's different. Ellie is a diminutive. A pet name."

"Will you please stop the car! We're already past it."

"Past what?"

"My shop. I want to pick up a plant."

"Ellie, this isn't the time—"

"Trust me."

Patrick flipped on the intercom and asked the driver to stop. He accompanied Elinor to her shop, gently complaining as they went. Once they were inside, he felt that old familiar calmness that came with the warm, moist atmosphere and flower-scented air.

"Roses, do you think, or—" A devilish smile lit her face. "No, let's give him a cactus."

"Whom are we honoring with this tribute?"

"Rosco, of course. I need some excuse to get a key from the cleaning staff. I'll tell them I'm delivering a plant to Rosco. Is that his first name or his last?"

"Rosco Devine, and if you leave your calling card, he'll know exactly who visited him."

She gave an impish grin. "Sweet revenge. If he visited my apartment uninvited, I wouldn't mind letting him know I returned the compliment."

"You didn't used to be vengeful. Leave him a bill for the cactus," Patrick suggested, and they laughed.

It seemed incredible they were laughing at such a troubled moment, but there was a happy excitement in just being together again. In a way, Elinor was enjoying the escapade more than sitting in state at a fancy restaurant. They returned to the car and were soon at the hotel. Patrick directed the chauffeur to the underground parking lot.

"Stand by, Ron," he told the chauffeur. "If all goes well, I'll be wanting you again in ten minutes. Make yourself inconspicuous in a dim corner of the lobby, okay?"

Ron tipped his hat and left. "First stop, the front desk," Elinor said. "Oh, good, I know the attendant. You keep the plant for now."

"Aren't you going to use that as an excuse to visit Rosco's room?"

"Don't be silly. They don't give delivery people the key. You have to leave the plant for the staff to deliver. They probably won't even give me the room number. If I can find out, we can call up to Rosco's room and make sure he's not there."

"Then why did we bring the plant along? And how do we get in?"

"If I find a friendly bellboy on duty, I'll offer to save him a trip upstairs. I've done it a few times before when they were busy. They're plenty busy tonight, from the looks of things."

Elinor went to the registration desk and talked with the clerk for a few minutes between customers. While the clerk was busy, Elinor flipped through the registry and got Rosco Devine's room number: 718. That was to the left of the elevator. She nodded to Patrick and he joined her. "Seven-eighteen," was all she said.

"Good work. I'll call to make sure Rosco isn't having a snooze." He used the lobby phone, holding it so they could both hear the repeated buzzes. "That's six rings. He can't be there."

"Then I'll make a quick trip to the staff's quarters and see what's shaking," Elinor said. "I'll need the plant."

"Should I wait here?"

"No, meet me on the seventh floor. I'll be using the service elevator, with any luck."

She took the cactus and hurried to the warren of housekeeping rooms below stairs, where guests never ventured but where the domestic arrangements for their comfort were executed. She went to a large room off the kitchen. It was a hive of activity that night. The intercom was a whole wall of numbered lights from the various rooms. It was lit up with orders. She said a few words to the busy housekeeper.

Elinor chatted for a minute to one of the bellboys she knew. By listening to what was going on around her, she discovered who was on service for the seventh floor. It was a young man named Arnie. Unfortunately she didn't know him, but when he went to the kitchen to pick up an order of sandwiches and coffee, she went with him.

"I have this delivery for the seventh floor," she said, smiling. "You look loaded down with that tray. I'll go along with you. You can let me into 718, okay?"

"Sure," he said, grinning. "It'll save me another trip. But we share tips, deal?"

"Yeah, if there's anybody there. If not, I'll just leave the plant."

When the elevator opened at the seventh floor, she saw Patrick was already there, walking slowly down the hall, looking at room numbers. She pretended not to recognize him. "Here's room 718," she said to the bellboy.

After knocking, he unlocked it, peered into a dark room and said, "Darn. No tip. Make sure you close the door when you come out."

"Sure." She waved and went in. "Mr. Devine, delivery," she called twice. When there was no answer, she turned on the light and saw the room was empty. The door to the bathroom was open, and she could see that it, too, was empty.

When the bellboy turned the corner, Elinor opened the door wide and saw Patrick gliding swiftly down the hall toward her. He slipped in and they closed the door. Excitement and fear lent a certain anxiety to the affair. Elinor's heart pounded, but she willed herself to remain calm. They looked all around before beginning the search. The room had been tidied. The bed was made, but a clutter of papers lay on top of it. Patrick hurried forward.

"I'll check his luggage," Elinor said, and went to the closet. When she saw that the soft-walled case was unlocked, she had a fair idea the letters weren't inside but she looked anyway. They weren't there. They weren't on the top shelf of the closet or in any of the various dresser and desk drawers.

"Did you find anything?" she asked Patrick.

"Nothing relevant. He must have them with him." They looked around the room again, searching for hiding places. It was Patrick who discovered the briefcase, hidden under the bed. "Maybe not!" He grinned, pulling it out. He put it on the bed and examined it. It held work papers but no letters.

"He wouldn't have carried a big parcel of letters like that in his hands," Elinor mused. "They were too bulky to hide in his jacket pocket. He'd have taken them in the briefcase if he took them at all. Let's look under the mattress."

"That's a woman's hiding place," Patrick objected.

"Maybe he got smart and thought like a woman. Lift."

They each took one end of the mattress and lifted. The pristine white mattress cover held no letters. They jiggled the mattress back into place and sat on the edge of the bed.

"Think," Elinor urged. "Where could they be?"

"In an oilskin bag in the water tank in the bathroom?" he suggested, half joking, but he went and looked.

"Maybe he doesn't have them," she said pensively.

"If he had them, they'd be here. I doubt if he'd trust them to the mail. He'd keep them near him. I know he didn't drive his own car so they can't be there. He came with a group in a rented limo. And you said, he wouldn't carry such a bulky bundle in his bare hands, and since his briefcase is here it looks like we've been wasting our time."

"In that case, I'm not leaving him my cactus," she said, and picked it up. "Better douse the lights," she added as they prepared to leave. "Where do we go now?"

"Some place quiet to rethink this thing."

"The coffee shop?"

"I was thinking of my room. It's close, on the eighth floor."

"Oh!" It seemed rather suggestive, going to a bachelor's hotel room. "Now, that would be really incriminating, if anyone happened to see us. Aspiring congressman in love tryst with strange lady."

A smile crinkled the edge of his eyes. "You're not that strange," he said. "Lots of people date hibiscuses. I know a guy who goes out with a rubber tree, or he did till she gave him the bounce."

"That's a terrible joke. And I meant mysterious, as you very well know."

He leaned closer. "But did you really mean *love* tryst, Ellie? Love is the operative word here."

She gulped and was aware with awful certainty that she was blushing. "You carry the cactus," she said, thrusting it at him so suddenly that the needles pricked his fingers. "And I'll turn out the lights."

"Good."

While they spoke, there was a sound at the door—unmistakably the sound of a key entering a lock. They looked at each other in mute horror. There wasn't even time to turn off the lights. The switch was right beside the door.

"Duck!" Patrick whispered, and they both dived behind the bed.

Chapter Five

A moment's pause told them this was a poor hiding place. They exchanged a look, then ran together to the clothes closet. Just as Patrick drew the door partially closed behind them, the door to the hallway opened and a man came in. Through the narrow opening, Elinor saw a heavyset, balding man in a dark suit.

She didn't know whether she was more embarrassed or afraid. If she'd been alone she would have been petrified, but with Patrick she felt more secure. It occurred to her that Rosco might be here for the night, in which case she and Patrick had a major problem on their hands. She looked at her partner in crime, wondering if this had occurred to him. A bar of light from the partially open door slanted along his face. She couldn't be sure, but he looked as if he was smiling. Suddenly the situation seemed funny to her.

As she watched, Rosco went to the bed and began riffling through the papers there. A voice suddenly called in from the doorway. "Get the lead out, Rosco. Thornby's waiting."

"Hold your horses," Rosco replied, and the other man came into the room. He was taller, thinner and more intelligent looking than Rosco. "Now, where'd I put that report?" Rosco muttered.

"Where's your briefcase?" the thin man asked.

"It's not in there. It's here somewhere." He continued shuffling his papers. "I think this is it." He picked up a folder and took it closer to the light.

"So what do you think old Firth's up to?" the other man asked.

Elinor felt Patrick's fingers tighten on her arm. He'd be interested to hear this conversation.

"It looks like they're dumping Gower. Too bad for us. He was a sitting duck, once we started leaking a few tales. Thornby could have taken him easily."

"That's why they dumped him. You think they'll go with Barron?"

Rosco answered in a jeering voice. "Who else? Mr. Movie Star's become Firth's right-hand man."

Elinor grinned and squeezed back on Patrick's arm.

"That's too bad. I've never heard a whisper of anything sordid in his life. I'll have to start digging. Nobody could be as clean as he looks at first glance. There's got to be something in his past. We'll start with his academic background. Lots of these guys have hazy memories of their college days. Funny they never imagine their *C*s were *F*s. They were always *A*s."

No problem there, Elinor noted. She had seen Patrick's curriculum vitae. Not straight *A*s, but nothing below a *B*.

"Yeah," Rosco said over his shoulder. "And then there's women. They're worse than faked college grades. They've got louder voices." He laughed at his puny joke. "With a face like Barron's, the women must be all over him."

The papers rustled, and footsteps receded toward the door. Rosco switched out the lights as he left. Apparently he hadn't noticed they'd been on when he entered.

In the darkness, Elinor breathed a sigh of relief. "That was close! Let's get out of here while the getting's good."

They left the closet but not the room. "We'll wait till they've caught the elevator. You realize what that conversation means?" Patrick asked.

"Of course. It means they don't have the letters. And we went through this for nothing. What it *doesn't* tell us is who has them. Got any ideas?"

"Plenty." His hands reached for her, still in the darkness, and when he spoke, his voice was a seductive purr. "A dark hotel room, me... you—all over me. I must admit I like the idea." His arms closed around her waist. The nibbling kisses he traced down her jaw left a fiery trail of tingles.

Elinor felt that weakening lethargy invade her bones, and she pulled herself back to the job at hand. "My main idea is to get out of here, in case Rosco and friend decide to come back."

He pulled her more tightly against him, while a low chuckle reverberated in his throat. "Don't be nervous. Maybe I should turn on the light, so you can fall victim to my charm," he teased.

"When you've seen one movie star's face, you've seen them all," she said, striving for a breezy air. "I always preferred brains myself."

"I have a few of those, too," he reminded her.

She began tugging at his arms to free herself. In the darkness, she felt them tighten, pulling her against the strength of his chest. Its warmth and his closeness began to affect her senses. While she could still speak, she asked nonchalantly, "Where's my cactus?"

"You don't need a cactus. You're prickly enough." The gibe was uttered in a caressing tone that made it sound like a compliment. His chin rubbed against her forehead. He was going to kiss her. While the prospect thrilled her, this didn't seem either the time or place for it.

Elinor abruptly moved to the bedside table and switched on the light. "Did we leave any other clues?" she asked, with a quick, businesslike look around the room. "I guess not."

Patrick gave her a dissatisfied look and picked up the cactus. Elinor turned off the lamp, and they slipped quietly out into the hallway. "My place?" Patrick asked. It was half a question, half an invitation.

"Why your place? Do you think there might be a ransom note for the letters? That's top priority at the moment, isn't it?"

"As I said earlier and unfortunately forgot—business before pleasure," he agreed. "Since our attempt at burglary didn't work out, I have a few phone calls to make. I'd rather make them from my room than in a crowded lobby. But if you'd rather not go with me, you can wait with Ron in the lobby."

His suggesting a convenient place to wait sounded as if he didn't really want her present for the phone calls. "Will you be long?" she asked.

"Five minutes should do it."

"Do you have another idea about who might have the letters?"

"Yes, an even likelier thief than Rosco has just occurred to me. I'll tell you about it when I meet you. Your turn to baby-sit the cactus," he said, handing it to her.

Elinor went downstairs, wondering whom Patrick was calling. "An even likelier thief than Rosco," he had said. It couldn't be anyone connected with Harry Thornby's campaign, or Rosco would have known about it. So who could it be? In the lobby, she spotted the wide shoulders and uniform of the chauffeur. She joined him in his inconspicuous corner.

"Mr. Barron will be here in a minute," she said. "Sorry to keep you waiting, Ron. Do you mind if I call you Ron? I don't know your other name."

"Ron Savage, but I'd be happy if you called me Ron," he said, smiling and offering his huge hand.

She was surprised to see he had the battered face of a boxer. It hadn't been evident earlier, in the shadows of night. His nose had obviously been broken and never properly reset. He also had a scar over his left cheekbone. That face, along with his burly build, suggested that he was an ex-boxer. He seemed an even more unsuitable politician's helper than Rosco Devine. Maybe he was Firth's bodyguard as well as driver.

"I'm Elinor Waring," she said.

"Would you mind telling me why you're carrying around that plant, Miss Waring? If it isn't a secret, I mean."

Not knowing how much the chauffeur could be trusted, she made a vague reply. "I had planned to give it to someone as a present."

"Is it bugged?" he asked.

Her eyes widened in astonishment. "No, of course not."

"The reason I asked, if it's for any of Thornby's party, that old chestnut wouldn't work. But I guess Mr. Barron wouldn't be that dumb. He seems like a pretty sharp guy."

Elinor began to realize that politics had something in common with crime. Stealing private correspondence and breaking into people's rooms and now a casual mention about bugging. To say nothing of Firth having a bodyguard—if Ron was a bodyguard. She asked him.

"I take care of Mr. Firth," he replied blandly. "I don't have to use my fists very often in this job, but if necessary, I can still handle most comers. Since we're getting personal, would you mind telling me what's going on, Miss Waring? Firth doesn't usually lend the limo to his staff. Mr. Barron must be on to something. I'd like to help, is why I'm asking."

Elinor felt that if Patrick wanted the chauffeur to know, he'd tell him. She even wondered if Ron was completely trustworthy. He seemed awfully curious for a chauffeur. "I wouldn't know. We're just friends," she replied.

Ron regaled Elinor with a few exploits from his past while they waited for Patrick to return. The incidents, if not actually illegal, sounded highly immoral. She didn't trust him an inch.

It wasn't much more than five minutes till Patrick came. "Ready when you are," he said to Elinor. To the chauffeur he added, "Do you know where the Trattoria Vespucci is?"

"I'll have to check at the desk," Ron told him.

"I know where it is," Elinor said. "It's right on the main street, at the western edge of town."

"Could you handle fettuccine about now?" Patrick asked her. "I sure could. I'm so tired of the rubber chicken and Styrofoam beef circuit I'd appreciate some real food."

Elinor glanced at her watch. She wasn't used to eating a second dinner at eleven-thirty, but she said, "I can handle a few antipasti, at least, and maybe a glass of Chianti."

"I'll bring the car around to the front," Ron said.

"We'll go to the parking lot with you," Patrick countered, and handed him the cactus. "No point in advertising that we're leaving. Someone might be curious enough to follow, and we may have a few detours to make before the night's over."

Elinor would have preferred a few minutes of total privacy with Patrick. She wanted to ask him whether

Ron was completely trustworthy. When they were in the back seat, she glanced at the glass partition. After Ron's remark about the plant's being bugged, even that barrier wasn't enough security. Ron might easily have the back seat bugged, if he was working for Thornby.

"Well, aren't you going to ask me how the calls went?" Patrick said as the car glided out of the parking lot.

She gave him a warning look. "Later."

He looked at her in confusion. "Why later? I thought you'd want to know who—"

"You'll love the Trattoria," she said in a rather loud voice. "But unless you're a real fettuccine nut, I recommend the veal parmigiana. Oh, and the pâté! You have to try Maria's pâté."

She raved about the menu, while Patrick listened in confusion. When the limousine glided up in front of the restaurant and Ron held the door, she hurried beyond earshot. "I didn't want you to say anything in front of Ron. I don't trust him, Patrick. He was asking an awful lot of questions. He might have the back seat of that limo bugged. You'd better check it."

"And I thought *I* was suspicious!" He laughed. "Ron is like Firth's son—or Caesar's wife. You have to have top security clearance for that job."

"There's no point taking chances," she warned. "I feel as if I'd landed in the middle of Deltagate."

He smiled down at her. "I had mentally christened this caper Elliegate."

Elinor tossed her head in mock annoyance, but in fact she felt mildly honored. They entered the restaurant. The Trattoria was one of the finer eateries in Delta. Candlelight flickered on linen-covered tables, and the discreet clink of cutlery and wineglasses melded with low conversations. The crowd was thinning at that hour, but about half the tables were still occupied. A violinist played softly romantic music in a far corner of the room. He didn't pester the patrons by touring their tables but provided unobtrusive background music.

"A nice place," Patrick said, glancing around.

"I wonder who does their flowers," Elinor said.

He gave her a mock frown. "I see you're in a mood for romance."

Elinor noticed that it *was* a romantic choice of place for a late night dinner. This evening had begun on a hectic note, but she felt it would terminate much more enjoyably. The maître d' approached them.

"Miss Eliot's table, please," Patrick said.

Jane Eliot! So that's why they were here. And she thought this was to be a romantic interlude! Miss Eliot had apparently warned the waiter she was expecting company. They were ushered to her table immediately. She sat alone, but the waiters were clearing away dishes from three other places, indicating that she hadn't dined alone.

As they all greeted one another politely, Elinor noticed that in fancy clothes and by candlelight, Jane Eliot looked very attractive. That elegant black dress made her look sophisticated. Just how close were she and Patrick? How had he known she was dining here, anyway?

Jane turned to Patrick and said, "You were fast, Barron. I don't think the other reporters have got a whiff of the letters yet."

Elinor felt a sting of anger that he had taken Jane into his confidence.

Jane continued, "Naturally I didn't say anything to give it away, but a vague hint as to why Firth chose you did the trick. They all agreed your character is untarnished sterling. Such a pleasant change," she said, smiling with admiration. "But of course you'll make very dull copy for us!" Her pout had a coquettish air.

Patrick regarded her with a leery eye. "It wasn't really the others I was worried about, Jane. It was you."

"I'm flattered!"

"You were the only one who knew that Elinor and I—that I was Elinor's friend."

"And even I didn't know there were love letters involved," she pointed out, with a brightly curious eye directed at Elinor. "You assured me you and Miss Waring were just friends. The friendship wasn't entirely platonic, I take it?"

"Couples at that age aren't much into philosophy," he said. "Although I did happen to quote Plato to ill effect."

"Poor choice!" Jane laughed.

Elinor felt out of it. Patrick had mentioned something about Plato and communism earlier. It was news to her if communism had been around in ancient Greece.

"Just how hot are these letters?" Jane asked, eyes sparkling with interest.

"The paper didn't spontaneously combust," Elinor said sharply, then added, "Unfortunately. That would have solved all our problems."

Jane leaned her elbows on the table and became very businesslike. "Let's get down to the journalists' five basics. Who, what, when, where, why? Who'd want them? Thornby's crew. What? Obviously the letters. When?" She looked from one to the other.

Elinor said, "They were taken sometime between 8:30 this morning, when I left for work, and 6:10 tonight, when I returned. And the where is from my apartment."

"And where is that, exactly?" Jane demanded.

"Maple Drive, but Rosco Devine was the only man who could possibly have known that, and he didn't have the letters."

Jane shook her head. "Don't be absurd, Miss Waring. Everybody in Thornby's party probably knows by now. They're dogging Barron's every step. Word's out that he's going to be the candidate. Now, about the why of snatching the letters. That answers itself. To smear Barron."

Elinor's blood began to simmer. "I'm not a monster, you know! Love letters to me will hardly ruin Patrick!"

Jane gave her a disparaging look. "Wake up and smell the scandal, Miss Waring. A laundry list can be manipulated to make the writer *look* like a bad risk. Phrases taken out of context, misinterpreted." She turned to Patrick, and her expression softened. "All right, I'll help you, Barron. But remember, when you're elected, you owe me. I'll get on it right away. And now I really must leave you two... friends?''

She gave a coy laugh, took her purse and turned away. But before she left she added over her shoulder, ''I'll be meeting the press crew back at the hotel, in that little bar.'' It sounded like an invitation—to Patrick. He was the one she was speaking to.

Elinor was glad she had left, but a sense of resentment lingered. ''You didn't mention why we were coming here,'' she said rather stiffly.

''You didn't give me much chance. You were busy warning me against the chauffeur.''

''Well, maybe I should just warn you against Ms. Eliot while I'm at it. The woman's a reporter, for heaven's sake! Why do you think she's so eager to involve herself? She'll have those letters all over the newspaper if she beats us to them.''

''No, we agreed she hands them over to me and writes nothing.''

''Why would she do that?'' The only reason Elinor could think of was that Miss Eliot and Patrick were very good friends indeed.

''Reporters like to have an inside track with politicians. It can give them the lead on a good story at times. Politicians and reporters are natural bedfellows.''

She leveled a cool stare at him. ''I was beginning to get that idea.''

He grinned. ''Don't take that literally. Jane's a bright woman. She has a network of connections reaching from here to Beijing. She'll be the first to get wind of anything, and she'll let me know before it hits the press."

Elinor sighed wearily. "I'm beginning to wonder if I didn't imagine the whole thing. Did those letters ever exist, or did I dream that stack of envelopes, tied up in pink ribbon?"

The eyes gazing at her held a laughing sparkle. "Pink ribbon, huh? Mine are bound up in a lacy garter I snagged at a wedding. Some Freudian thought afoot there, do you think?"

It was too late to deny the pink ribbon, so Elinor had to remove the suggestion of caring. "You'd better burn them. Receiving love letters is probably open to misinterpretation, too."

"Yours weren't dangerously passionate," he said. "I always had the feeling you were holding back." His eyebrows rose in an unspoken question.

"Wasn't that discreet of me? And I didn't even have any political ambitions."

"You're still holding back your feelings," he said with a searching look.

"You're right. Maybe I'm holding back too much. I don't much care for any of this, Patrick. I don't like that you phoned, pretending you wanted to see me, when all you wanted was your letters. I don't like that our date has become a treasure hunt, and I don't particularly relish the idea that someone's following me, breaking into my apartment. In fact, I don't like being with you anymore. I'm going home. And don't bother calling your limousine, which is probably bugged. I don't know how you can live in an atmosphere of distrust and treachery like this. I'll call a cab."

Patrick looked taken aback but soon recovered. "I should be more careful what I say to you. You really let it all out that time. Ellie, I'm sorry. I had no idea any of this would happen. I *did* want to see you. It wasn't just to get the letters back, although I admit that was the main reason I called you." He reached for her hands and took them both in his.

Her heart sank at his admission. She had suspected it, but it still hurt to hear it confirmed. "You should just have told me on the phone what you wanted. I assure you I didn't have any particular attachment to your letters. I would have burned them."

He gave her a coaxing smile. "Pink ribbon and all? I don't think you would have kept them all this time if they hadn't meant *something* to you."

"I'd forgotten all about them."

"And me? Did you forget me, too? I thought of you every time I looked at a plant. An awful lot of people have plants in their offices nowadays." He sensed a softening in her attitude and pressed on. "I guess I have a lot of apologizing to do. In this life I'm living now, everyone is involved in politics. The good of the party always comes first. We live, eat, sleep, breathe politics. I forgot, for a minute, that all this is new to you. Being followed and having someone break into your apartment—that's all my fault, and I truly am sorry."

"I don't know how you can stand it."

"You get used to it. When the stakes are high, people will do almost anything. A guy has to protect himself. That's all I'm doing. I haven't turned into a monster, you know."

Elinor knew from his intense expression that he wanted her to understand and to forgive. "I guess that old political expression applies to me," she said uncertainly. "'If you can't stand the heat, get out of the kitchen.' Maybe it's time for me to get out of the kitchen and leave it to you pros."

Patrick looked disappointed, but he didn't try to talk her out of it. "I dragged you into this unintentionally, and if you want out, just say the word. This is how my life is, and it won't get any better as the election heats up, or after." He studied her closely, holding his breath for her decision. It was the worst possible time to become romantically involved. If he didn't have the sense to back off, maybe it would be just as well if Elinor did.

Elinor wavered. It was an opportunity to make a graceful exit. She could forgive him, say it didn't really matter and leave. She'd probably never see him again. She took a long, hard look, trying to make up her mind. Was she really that much of a chicken that she couldn't take a little breaking and entering? Was she too stupid to outwit a man like Rosco Devine, who didn't even have the sense to realize someone had entered his room and turned on his lights? Was she inferior to Jane Eliot?

No way! With all Patrick's busy, bothersome life, she still wanted him. His methods might be questionable at times, but she had total confidence in his motives. Patrick had always been interested in saving the world, at whatever cost to himself. Sometimes the cost trickled down to those near to him. If she and Patrick were to have any future, she'd have to learn to accept that. And what he was saying did seem to imply at least the possibility of a future together for them.

"We'd better put on our thinking caps and find out who stole the letters," she said matter-of-factly. "If it wasn't Thornby's crew and it wasn't the press, who could it be?"

Patrick exhaled a silent sigh of relief. A smile softened his rugged features, and his eyes glowed. "Maybe it *was* the press. Jane will keep an ear to the ground for us. I don't see who else it could have been. My own party wouldn't have done it. Party unity is top priority. There wasn't anything else taken from your apartment, was there? I mean, it couldn't have been an ordinary burglar."

"Nothing else was gone."

"Then it was a reporter," he decided. "Someone followed us last night when we left the hotel. And now that we've decided that, let's forget business and enjoy what's left of our date."

"Actually, I still have a question. How did you know Miss Eliot was here? That's who you phoned from the hotel, was it?" She tried not to make it sound like an accusation.

Apparently she succeeded. He answered easily. "Yes, I called Jane. It was beginning to seem that our thief was a reporter, and she can find that out more easily and more quickly than I can. All the reporters eat here. She mentioned this afternoon that it had terrific fettuccine. That's why I suggested it."

His answer didn't reveal anything except that he'd been talking to Jane Eliot that afternoon. His easy answer made it sound innocent of anything but business.

He picked up the menu. "The veal parmigiana, I think you recommended?"

"And Chianti."

He squeezed her fingers. "Don't you think, for this occasion—champagne?"

"Not with Italian food. I think I will order a full meal, though. This life of crime whets the appetite."

"It's the quickened pace," he said. "It has that effect of increasing the appetite." When he looked at her like that, Elinor didn't think it was only his appetite for food that was heightened. The tension between them was growing, too.

The wine arrived first, and they sipped it while talking. "This is sure different from the old days, isn't it?" Elinor said. "Do you remember the pizza and beer we used to get at Luigi's in the Village?"

He laughed. "One beer, nursed slowly so it'd last through dinner. They were good times."

"Do you ever feel...I don't know, not guilty exactly but sort of indulged, to be able to order champagne whenever you want and have that big limo waiting for you? It seems so capitalistic."

"Nope. America's a capitalist country and proud of it. I work about eighteen hours, most days. I figure I earn a few perks. The limo isn't mine, it's Firth's. Public figures have a certain dignity to uphold. I wouldn't want the rest of the world to see my congressman riding in a taxi, would you?"

"No, I guess not."

"Elected politicians represent the people and the American dream. As long as they don't lose sight of the fact that plenty of people are walking—with holes in their shoes—I don't think anyone begrudges his representative the use of a car and chauffeur. Besides, it's practical. A lot of work goes on in the rear seat of that limousine. It doesn't always carry champagne. Aspirins and a load of paperwork is more like it. But we're not going to talk shop tonight. We're going to talk about us."

A pungent aroma of oregano and garlic wafted from the steaming plate of veal. While they ate, it was easy to slip into the old familiarity. Elinor thought the man across from her, candlelight flickering over the severe planes of his lean face, hadn't changed much. His hair was barbered more carefully and his jacket was downright exquisite. A few fine lines were beginning to invade his forehead, but he was basically the same man, with the same ideals.

Patrick talked eloquently about his plans for helping the underprivileged. That was always his chief concern, that the poor, especially the young, be given a chance. He talked about schools and housing and welfare. She thought he didn't even notice that he was talking shop again, but he checked himself a little later.

"Why didn't you put a muzzle on me?" he asked in chagrin. "Let's talk about you instead. Have you met any interesting plants lately?"

"A whole family named *Cactaceae*."

"You must introduce me. We Democrats have traditionally got the ethnic vote. I wouldn't want to lose them. But seriously, are you into cactuses now? You never kept them before. They're so . . . prickly."

"They're not my own favorite choice, but I have to stock what the customers want."

He nodded. "Even in your idyllic job, realism has reared its ugly head, huh?"

"Well, it *is* a job. And naturally I don't actively dislike *any* plant. I'm seeing an upsurge of sales in cactuses. Or cacti, depending on your views of Latin. I figure it's because people are too busy to water their plants regularly and want something that doesn't need a lot of attention. It's interesting, though, that they still want *something* living in their house. Besides other people, obviously."

Patrick listened with interest. "What do you think about silk plants? Bad news for you, I imagine?"

She huffed indignantly. "If people want sculpture, why not buy a statue? Silk plants are not living things. They're expensive, they fade in the sunlight, they're harder to dust than real plants and they never change. How boring, to have a plant never surprise you. That's half the pleasure of growing them. You notice I didn't say 'owning' them? We don't 'own' plants. We adopt them."

"I thought you were going to say they own us—like cats."

"No, they're totally dependent, more like children. And wonderful like children, too, in their way. The first time my old jade flowered, it was like—I don't know. Like a miracle, sort of. It grew for ten years without a flower, then one winter it burst into tiny white blossoms. And vines will often do it, too. Even ivies."

Patrick grinned at her enthusiasm. "Just when you think you know someone..." he said, with a meaningful look. "But with plants, unlike people, it seems the surprises are invariably delightful."

"Far from it!" she objected. "They're as likely as not to start turning yellow and dropping leaves on you. Even when they're properly fed and illuminated and debugged and everything. They just get sick. There's still a lot we don't know about plants."

He inclined his head. "Maybe they're lonesome, deprived of congenial... friends?" His tone suggested he meant something else. "I feel a few leaves sagging myself. What do you say we go home, Ellie?"

"I guess I really didn't want dessert. Although they have delicious spumoni here."

"It doesn't go with champagne. We still have that waiting in the car."

"I have some chocolate ripple ice cream in the fridge at home."

Amusement beamed in the depth of his dark eyes. "Now, that would go with champagne!"

She gave him a rueful look. "All right, I get the idea, Patrick. You want to leave. You're tired and you want to go to b—home," she said, pulling herself up short on the word.

"You were right the first time." He gave her a laughing look and signaled for the bill.

In the back seat of the limousine, they held hands and she leaned her head on his shoulder. "I suppose you're tied up all day tomorrow?'' she asked, feeling gypped.

"I've managed to wiggle out of a few things. I told Firth about the letters. I felt I owed it to him. He suggested I make recovering them my first priority, so you'll be hearing from me."

When they stopped in front of Elinor's apartment, Ron opened the car door for them and said, "Do you want me to stick around, Mr. Barron?"

Patrick took the bottle of champagne from the ice bucket. "I'll take a cab home, Ron. Thanks."

The chauffeur gave a thirsty smile at the bottle, said, "Have one for me," and handed Elinor the cactus. Then he hopped back into the car and drove off.

Elinor disliked that grin and said, "I wouldn't trust him an inch. If I were you, I'd check up on old Ron and see what he was up to all day when the letters were stolen."

Patrick just shook his head. "Next you'll be saying Firth took them. You can't allow yourself to become totally cynical, even in politics. You have to know who to trust. Ron's okay. He's just a diamond in the rough."

"He's in a perfect position to spy for Thornby. If he bugged the back seat, he'd hear all kinds of stuff."

"That's why the FBI investigates drivers very carefully before hiring them, Ellie."

They began the climb upstairs. "If you say so, but don't say I didn't warn you, if he turns out to be the mole."

"Mole? This is not a case of international espionage."

When they went to her apartment door, he said, "Did you get that lock changed?"

"I forgot all about it."

"Do it tomorrow, will you?"

"That's known as locking the barn door after the horses have bolted, isn't it?"

"There's something more valuable than letters in this apartment." He studied her for a long moment.

She nodded her head, pretending to misunderstand him. "You're right. I'd feel terrible if anyone kidnapped my plants."

FIRST-CLASS ROMANCE

Mail This Heart TODAY!

And We'll Deliver:

**4 FREE BOOKS
A FREE DIGITAL
CLOCK/CALENDAR
PLUS A SURPRISE
MYSTERY BONUS
TO YOUR DOOR!**

See Inside For More Details

SILHOUETTE® DELIVERS FIRST-CLASS ROMANCE— DIRECT TO YOUR DOOR

Mail the Heart sticker on the postpaid order card today and you'll receive:

—4 new Silhouette Romance™ novels—FREE
—a lovely lucite digital clock/calendar—FREE
—and a surprise mystery bonus—FREE

But that's not all. You'll also get:

Free Home Delivery

When you subscribe to Silhouette Romance™, the excitement, romance and faraway adventures of these novels can be yours for previewing in the convenience of your own home. Every month we'll deliver 6 new books right to your door. If you decide to keep them, they'll be yours for only $1.95* each and there is *no* extra charge for postage and handling! There is no obligation to buy—you can cancel at any time simply by writing ''cancel'' on your statement or by returning a shipment of books to us at our cost.

Free Monthly Newsletter

It's the indispensable insider's look at our most popular writers and their upcoming novels. Now you can have a behind-the-scenes look at the fascinating world of Silhouette! It's an added bonus you'll look forward to every month!

Special Extras—FREE

Because our home subscribers are our most valued readers, we'll be sending you additional free gifts from time to time in your monthly book shipments as a token of our appreciation.

OPEN YOUR MAILBOX TO A WORLD OF LOVE AND ROMANCE EACH MONTH. JUST COMPLETE, DETACH AND MAIL YOUR FREE-OFFER CARD TODAY!

*Terms and prices subject to change without notice.

Remember! To receive your free books, digital clock/calendar and mystery gift, return the postpaid card below. But don't delay!

DETACH AND MAIL CARD TODAY.

If offer card has been removed, write to:
Silhouette Books, 901 Fuhrmann Blvd., P.O. Box 1867, Buffalo, NY 14269-1867

MAIL THE POSTPAID CARD TODAY!

BUSINESS REPLY CARD

First Class   Permit No. 717   Buffalo, NY

Postage will be paid by addressee

Silhouette Books®
901 Fuhrmann Blvd.
P.O. Box 1867
Buffalo, NY 14240-9952

NO POSTAGE
NECESSARY
IF MAILED
IN THE
UNITED STATES

Chapter Six

"Your plant friends look fine to me," Patrick said as he entered and glanced around the gardenlike living room. He put the champagne on the desk and inhaled the sweet air as he took off his coat. "They have an enviable atmosphere. I always feel I'm on some lush tropical isle when I'm at your place."

"Moisture's good for people, too," Elinor replied. "Buildings get so dry in winter. I have two humidifiers just in this little apartment. That reminds me, I have to fill them. Just make yourself at home, Patrick."

When she had removed her coat, she pulled off her boots and slid into a pair of comfortable shoes.

For his part, Patrick wasn't used to being abandoned when he visited a woman, and he especially wasn't used to plants taking precedence over him. He noticed that even the bottle of champagne, rapidly warming on the desk, wasn't enough to lure her from her job. Ellie was never one to put on airs. He was glad she was treating him like an old friend, with no formality.

"Where would I find wineglasses?" he asked when she came in carrying a big watering can to fill the humidifier.

"The cupboard over the sink."

"Let me help you with that," he said, jumping up to take the watering can from her. It was surprisingly heavy. His shoulder sagged with the unexpected weight.

Elinor went in front of him to remove the grate from the top of the humidifier. He immediately began pouring from the can and was rewarded with a splash of water that shot up in his face, liberally wetting his jacket in the process.

"Let me shut it off first!" she exclaimed. "Didn't you see the fan turning?"

He had heard the whirring of the engine but hadn't realized the fan was exposed. He set the watering can down and mopped his face before whisking at the water on his jacket. "It seems poor manners aren't limited to politics. I don't like to speak ill of an inanimate object, but that humidifier is a boor."

"I hope you haven't wrecked the motor!" Elinor ignored his plight as she shut the machine off and poured the water herself. "I guess I don't have to change the water softener yet," she said, peering into the depths of the tank. "I see the tablet is still there. Would you mind putting the grate back on?"

He positioned the grate in the track and said, "Now that business is taken care of..." He looked meaningfully toward the champagne.

"There's another humidifier in my bedroom. It won't take a minute. Why don't you open the champagne while I fill it?"

"Wineglasses? Ah, cupboard over the sink."

"You might have to rinse them out. I hardly ever use them. They're probably dusty."

They were indeed dusty. "You lead a strangely uncivilized life, Elinor Waring," he said, shaking his head at the dusty glasses.

"Oh, it's not that I never drink champagne," she said over her shoulder as she filled the watering can. "It's just that I don't drink it here. It feels more like a celebration when I'm out someplace."

He wondered whom Elinor went out with to drink champagne. "I'll lug the can," he offered.

"It's okay. I'm used to it," she replied, and took it into the bedroom. Patrick followed, curious to see all the details of how she lived. He already realized her life-style was simple, relative to his own. But Elinor was intelligent. She could adapt to something more complex—if she wanted to.

The bedroom was like another hothouse, with plants hanging at the window and trailing from pots on the wall. While she filled the machine, he gazed all around. The room was modest but pretty. Her bed had a rattan headboard fashioned from trailing straw vines. The bureau and desk matched each other but not the bed. They were pine, trimmed with white porcelain knobs. He glanced at the paperback on her bedside table to see what she was reading. It was a mystery. Ellie had always liked mysteries.

On her bureau there was a collection of pictures. He peered to see if he was there and was disappointed to notice that he wasn't. What had she done with the silver-framed photograph he had given her one Christmas? At least he hadn't suffered the ultimate indignity of having his picture removed and something else put in the frame, because the frame wasn't there, either. He looked back at the bed. He couldn't imagine any orgies taking place under the crocheted afghan that served as a bedspread.

"My grandmother made that," she said, watching where he was looking. "She made it sixty years ago. It's beautiful, isn't it? All done by hand. She taught me how to crochet, but I never seem to have time for it. It's odd when you think of it. She had to do so much—help Grandpa tend the farm, make her own bread and everything—yet she found time to make things like this." She ran her fingers over it lovingly.

Elinor looked rather nostalgic. Patrick was aware that with most women, there would be some air of constraint at having him in their bedroom, so close to their bed. But there was none with Elinor, nor any sexual tension, either. The simple innocence of the room robbed the moment of that.

"I suppose it was the lack of TV that left their evenings free," he said.

"Yes, I remember it quite well. She used to sew and crochet in the evenings. She lived with us for a few years when Grandpa died. I have her picture here," she said, walking toward the bureau.

He gazed at an older woman. "You don't look much like her."

"I take after my mom. This is Dad's mother."

He examined the collection of photographs again, thinking he might be hidden at the rear. "These are all family members, are they?" he asked casually.

"Family and friends. This is my old schoolmate Annie Forrester," she said, pointing to a girl with pigtails and freckles.

Then it wasn't *all* family. That wasn't what accounted for his absence. "Anyone else I know?" he asked.

"You don't know Annie, do you?"

"Only by reputation. You used to mention her."

"Oh, I just wondered."

He looked down at her. "I think you know who I'm looking for."

Elinor read the question in his eyes. She cocked her head to one side and smiled mischievously. "I wonder if it could be the guy in my bottom drawer. He was hiding underneath a stack of letters last time I looked."

"Cut to the quick, Elinor. You've relegated me to the bottom drawer, like a poor relative. Why don't you give Patrick some of this lovely, soft air?"

"I do." Elinor strolled to the window, fingering a frond of a hanging plant. "Patrick is looking a little peaked," she said, and smiled over her shoulder at him. "Do you remember this asparagus fern?"

He looked at an enormous fall of spiky lace, with little bulblets of root pushing out of the pot. "I can't say that I do, but I'm very pleased to make his ac-

quaintance. Why was he named after me? Too big for
his breeches?'' he asked.

''You gave it to me. We were shopping one afternoon in the Village. There was a sidewalk stall selling
cut flowers and a few plants. You wanted to buy me
daffodils, but I talked you into this instead.''

''Good Lord!'' He stared at the plant as a tide of
memory engulfed him.

The day came rushing back. It had been spring, and
they had been going together for only a few months.
Bewitched by Elinor and the beauty of spring, he
wanted to buy her flowers. She had revised the romantic gesture by choosing a poor, wilting little plant
that looked ready for the trash can. And now it had
flourished into this beautiful thing.

''It even blossoms,'' she said proudly. ''After I put
it on the balcony last summer it became covered in little white flowers. That's where these little berries come
from. See, some of them were fertilized by bees or
butterflies and are already ripening from white to red.
I planted a few of them and got new plants. Your offspring.'' She laughed.

The playfully innocent mood was suddenly charged
with emotion. The memories of the past had started it,
but it was that casual mention of offspring that
brought it to a head. How much time had slipped
through their fingers! That stunted little plant, once
not more than six inches high, had grown into a veri-
table jungle. The plant had produced offspring—and
he and Ellie could have had children by now, if they
had...

He reached out and touched her lightly on the arm. "Elinor..."

Her breath was coming irregularly. She was suddenly very aware of the beckoning bed. Patrick wouldn't have suggested it in the old days, but they were older now. Fully mature adults. A touch of pink suffused her cheeks and she said briskly, "Let's have that champagne."

The moment passed, and they went into the living room for the ceremony of popping the cork. She noticed that Patrick had no trouble as his strong fingers expertly worked it loose without spilling a drop. There was a dainty pop as the cork flew onto the sofa. He had become so debonair since she used to know him. In his formal black suit and pouring the champagne, he looked utterly different from the man she used to date. How had he come such a long way in only three years? How had she remained so obdurately the same? She felt rather gauche beside him. She looked with dissatisfaction at her old shoes.

"Shall we propose a toast?" she suggested when he handed her the glass.

"To our offspring?" he suggested playfully. "I'd like to get one of them. Could I?"

"They're at home—on the farm, I mean." She didn't have room for them in her apartment, yet couldn't bear to completely part with them. "I'm afraid you'd be a neglectful parent. Plants require lots of attention."

"Perhaps visiting rights could be arranged?"

"Sure, between dinners and interviews and speeches. That would be about once a decade, huh?"

They sat down, and he reached for her hand again. This time she let him hold it. "A little more often than that, Ellie. Instead of regretting the past, why don't we enjoy the present?" He put down his glass and drew her into his arms.

She went reluctantly, feeling in her bones it was useless to resist. What worried her was not that she *didn't* care. It was that she cared too much. She wanted more from him than a few stray seconds stolen from work. But when he kissed her, a few stolen moments with Patrick seemed better than hours with anyone else. Her blood quickened, and when his lips moved hungrily on hers, she felt a lurch inside that soon swelled to a tumult.

She wrapped her arms around him. His arms tightened till he was crushing her against his chest as if he would never let her go. A pressure in her began building when his tongue flicked against her lips, nudging them open. Her arms rose and closed possessively around his neck, reveling in the remembered masculine feel and scent and touch of him. His hard body pressed the ripe invitation of her breasts. The rough smoothness of his jacket tingled against her flesh. She enjoyed the crisp richness of his hair under her fingers, the indefinable scent that was part spice, part musk and all charged with the emotion of remembered passion. It came sweeping over her, leaving her breathless.

When his hand moved to brush her throat, she felt a shudder of desire shake her. His fingers stroked gently, with engrossing intimacy, as they traced her jawline, then moved to enmesh themselves in her hair.

While he held her head, his tongue moved in her mouth with disturbing expertise, stroking, caressing and turning her to warm mush. Patrick had always been a masterful kisser. And in the old days he had always stopped there. She had a nervous feeling he didn't intend to stop at a kiss this time.

She was weakening. His hand began a persuasive massage of her breast, sending a flame of fire flashing through her veins. His fingers relaxed a moment, then splayed and caught the full mound, squeezing gently, with insistent sureness. His other hand left her head and lowered to pull her hips closer. She felt his tempting warmth along her body, urging her on to intimacy.

Elinor thought of what he had said. "Instead of regretting the past, why don't we enjoy the present?" But what about the future? What enjoyment would there be in having given herself to him, if that was all there was going to be between them? And he had made pretty clear that his schedule was tight for the next year. After that, he might be a congressman, with even more strenuous duties.

She withdrew her arms from his neck, braced her hands on his shoulders and pushed lightly. "That's enough enjoyment for one night," she said. Her voice was tinged with regret.

Patrick looked at her, surprised. "We've just begun! This is our first real kiss."

"And our last, for now. Let's have the champagne, before it goes flat." She reached for the glass and sipped. The bubbles rose slowly up from the side of the glass, bursting against her lips and tickling her nose. Champagne should induce a lovely, romantic mood, but she felt sad and cheated. "I don't have champagne very often," she said, knowing she was repeating herself.

"Is there an inference in there that making love is less unusual?" His lifted eyebrows and his dark eyes showed sharp interest.

Elinor stiffened her shoulders. "That's not what I meant."

He looked at her, a long, tension-filled look. He had no right to ask but felt incapable of leaving it alone. He had to know. "But do you? Make love, I mean?"

She couldn't decide whether she resented the question or liked that he was interested. "Do you?" she parried.

"Not often, but I'd be happy to make an exception. Now it's your turn."

"That depends on what you mean by 'making love.' I have boyfriends. I'm not intimate with them," she said bluntly. His eyebrows settled down, and a slow smile grew on his lips. It echoed in his glowing eyes. "No, when I make love, it'll be for keeps."

Patrick seized her hand and kissed the palm. "Amen."

"That wasn't a prayer, just a statement."

"A moral statement. A kind of prayer, in a way."

She sipped her wine again. "It doesn't seem right, drinking champagne and praying."

"That's because people have the idea that prayer and morality are bleak, without pleasure. That's not my view of life or morality."

"I know." It was true. Patrick had high morals, but they didn't deprive his life of fun. Again she thought of those walks in the snow. "Patrick," she said, on an impulse, "let's go out and walk in the snow."

He looked startled. "Why?"

"Just because—" *Because we used to, when we were in love.* But she couldn't say that. "I guess it'd be silly."

"And cold." He filled her glass and his own.

A silence grew, not one of the comfortable sort. Elinor felt a strangeness growing and spoke, just to break the tension. "I keep thinking about those letters. I wonder who took them."

"I keep thinking about that lock that couldn't keep a child out. I wish you'd push a chair or something in front of your door tonight and get it changed tomorrow."

"Don't worry, I will. If any other uninvited caller comes, he'll have to climb in the window." Patrick gave a jump of alarm. "Just kidding. I'm on the third floor."

A sharp rap sounded at the door, and before Elinor went to answer it, Gillie Parson peeped her head in. "I saw your light and thought you were alone. Sorry. I'll go." She looked at the champagne bottle and smiled hopefully.

"Don't be silly. Come on in and have a drink," Elinor said, and was relieved for the interruption. Patrick didn't look too happy, and for some reason, that made her feel good. She'd have to dust off another glass, but before going into the kitchen, she made the introductions.

From the kitchen, Elinor listened to their conversation.

"We've met—sort of," Gillie said. "You were at the TV station yesterday with Congressman Firth and Tony Gower, weren't you, Patrick?"

"Yes, I was." He smiled and didn't mention that he didn't recognize her.

"The man who interviewed you, Luke Williams, is my boyfriend," Gillie was saying. "Luke's very much interested in politics. He belongs to a party—officially, I mean. He contributes and everything."

"I was struck with his grasp of politics," Patrick said politely.

"He'd love to meet you more informally. Why don't we all get together some night?"

Elinor came back and poured the champagne. "Patrick is very busy," she said.

"Oh, I know how hard you guys work," Gillie said to Patrick. "Tony Gower was telling us about your schedule last night at the chamber of commerce ball."

Elinor said, "Gillie does a children's show at the station."

Gillie talked about it for a few minutes. "I hope you haven't forgotten you're doing the guest shot tomorrow," she reminded Elinor.

"I'll be there." She was really rather eager for Gillie to leave. "I'm glad you reminded me. I'll have to go to the shop and pick up the Christmas cactus."

"It's not like you to forget anything, Ellie," she teased. "I wonder what put it out of your mind?" She cast a meaningful look at Patrick. "I think I'm intruding," she said, and finished her drink. "See you at the station tomorrow. Don't forget!"

As soon as she left, Elinor turned to Patrick. "I'm sure you have a busy day tomorrow, too. Maybe we should call it a night."

"When your friend said Luke belonged to a party, I don't think she meant *my* party. It was Rosco they entertained last night. You don't think Gillie would have taken those letters for Luke?"

"No, absolutely not. She doesn't have a key."

"The door doesn't require a key. I imagine she has a credit card." He looked a question at her.

"You said at the restaurant that I was becoming a cynic, or you implied it. Gillie's a friend. She'd never do anything like that. You trust Ron. I trust Gillie. She has top-level clearance with me."

Patrick looked distracted a moment, but her words seemed to reassure him. "Then that clears her in my books, too. It was just a thought." He got up and took his coat from the chair.

Elinor wanted to ask if she'd see him tomorrow. He had mentioned having some time off to look for the letters, so maybe... But she decided not to ask. Her pride didn't want to give him the idea she was too eager.

"I'll have to call a taxi, since I sent Ron on ahead."

"I'll drive you back to the hotel, if you like."

"No, I'll call a cab."

She did it for him. "I'd better wait downstairs," he said. Elinor had thought they'd have a few more minutes together.

Patrick still seemed distracted when he left, though he gave her a light kiss on the cheek, and said "Sleep tight, darling."

While he waited for the taxi, Patrick pondered over Luke Williams and his friendship with Elinor. She trusted Gillie, but maybe Luke had arranged the snatch without Gillie's knowledge. If he was chummy with Rosco, it was worth looking into. . . .

Elinor knew she wouldn't sleep well, so she didn't even try to go to bed. There was too much on her mind. She thought their situation was bothering Patrick, too. He had certainly seemed preoccupied after Gillie left. Maybe he wasn't thinking of Elinor at all. He was probably just worried about the letters and losing the nomination. He didn't have it sewed up tight, although Firth was backing him, and that must mean a lot. But with Firth moving up to the Senate, maybe his influence in the Lower House wouldn't be that strong.

Patrick would make such a good representative. It would be a shame if someone like Gower got the nomination. It was guys like Gower who gave politics a bad name. She was beginning to feel a little giddy but didn't want to waste the champagne. She poured the last of it into her glass and sat down, thinking.

A man like Gower would probably pull all sorts of dirty tricks to win. He was as bad as Thornby's crew. An idea seemed to be niggling at the back of her mind. It was the champagne that was making her thinking fuzzy. She set the glass down and concentrated.

Who said it was the opposition that had stolen the letters? Tony Gower had an equally strong motive to discredit Patrick, and his reputation was shady. Patrick might talk about the good of the party always coming first, but she doubted if someone like Tony Gower was so idealistic. He hadn't been right here in the building last night like Rosco, but he'd seen her with Patrick at the hotel. In fact, he'd been hinting for an introduction.

It wouldn't be hard for him to find out who she was. Everyone at the hotel knew her name, and he could have got her address from the phone book. He could figure out that she'd be at her shop for most of the day. He could have gotten away from meetings for half an hour. That's all it would have taken.

The major flaw in her reasoning was that even if Tony Gower knew she was a friend of Patrick, he couldn't have known about the letters. Had he broken in, just looking around to see if he could find anything against her? Maybe he had come looking for drugs or some signs of sex or a sleazy life-style. Something to suggest that Patrick wasn't as simon-pure as everyone said.

She decided to call Patrick and tell him her suspicions. He wasn't in, so she left a message, thinking he'd be arriving any minute. In ten minutes, she called again. He had to be there by now.

The clerk tried his room, but there was no answer. Elinor left the message again, but after half an hour he still hadn't called. He hadn't gone back to the hotel at all. Where had he gone? An image of Jane Eliot popped into her head. "I'll be meeting the press crew back at the hotel, in that little bar." She had thought when Jane said it that it sounded like an invitation.

Was that why Patrick had agreed so readily that he had a busy day tomorrow? He had gone to the hotel all right, but he'd headed straight for the bar and Jane.

She dialed the hotel again and asked to have Mr. Barron paged at the bar. Within minutes, she heard his voice coming along the wire. "Barron here."

She hung up the phone softly. Tears stung her eyes, but she batted them away. It was nothing to get weepy about. He had a late date with Jane Eliot, that's all. What business was it of hers? None, and since he was having an affair with Jane Eliot, why the devil should she bother trying to help him find his letters? Let Gower show them to Firth. It seemed Patrick wasn't the angelic soul everyone took him for anyway.

Chapter Seven

Patrick phoned Elinor at her shop the next morning. "I hoped I'd catch you before you went to the TV station," he said. He didn't even have the conscience to sound guilty, and that annoyed her.

"Hello, Patrick. What can I do for you?"

"Say you're missing me as much as I'm missing you."

"That much?" She heard the ironic edge to her tone.

Apparently he noticed it, too.

"That's a lot, Ellie. I *do* miss you. I wish we could spend more time together. In fact, I've twisted Firth's arm and got some time off. I'll pick you up for lunch, though I'm afraid it'll have to be late. Are you free at one-thirty?"

Her heart hardened at his assumption that she'd arrange her life for his convenience. "A bad time for me, I'm afraid," she said, without even looking at her calendar.

"Damn. I have a business lunch at twelve, but I hoped—"

"And you planned to eat again at one-thirty? That'll play havoc with your boyish figure, Patrick."

"It wasn't actually the food I was looking forward to."

The insinuation in his speech began softening her resolve. She was still angry. She wouldn't give in on the lunch, but for old times' sake, she decided to warn him about Gower. "Actually, we should talk. I may have a lead on those letters. It's just an idea, but—"

"Good." He sounded interested but not totally intrigued. "Don't go doing anything dangerous in the way of recovering them. I may be on to something myself."

"Oh, really?"

"Yes, Jane Eliot came up with something. Trust Jane. She's wide-awake. A real go-getter. I was just talking to her."

"I see." Elinor's blood simmered. And you were talking to her last night, too. Funny you didn't mention that. I may be small-town, but I recognize a two-timer. "Say hi for me next time you see her." That'll probably be very soon.

"I'll do that."

"So, when do you think you might have a moment free—other than one-thirty, when I'm busy, that is? I imagine you want to hear my idea."

"I'll get back to you later this afternoon. Take care. Did you get that lock fixed?"

"I phoned the locksmith. He's very busy, but he's coming next week."

"You'd think the man was a politician!" He laughed.

"He'll probably be late, if he shows at all. If there's nothing else, Patrick, I have to get over to WHYM."

"Sorry. I'll call you later."

She hung up. He hadn't even asked what lead she had on the letters. Jane Eliot was on the case, and he obviously had more faith in the bright, ambitious Jane than in her. Her pride demanded that she teach him a lesson, but first she had to do this show for Gillie. She picked up the Christmas cactus and drove over to the station, rehearsing what she'd say. Gillie met her in the lobby and went with her to the makeup booth. She was wearing a bizarre bright red elf costume for the show in this Christmas season.

"I'm Santa's helper," Gillie said, crinkling her nose in derision. "Let's go and do our makeup."

The regulars did their own making up at this small station, and Elinor had appeared often enough that she did her own now, too.

"I hope my arrival last night didn't interrupt anything major," Gillie said. "I didn't realize you were dating Patrick Barron. Is it serious?"

Elinor managed to sound nonchalant. "No, not at all. He's much too busy for anything serious."

"All those politicians are. What a life they live. It's go, go, go all the time. Tony Gower was saying—"

Elinor gave a start of alarm. "Was he here?"

"Yes, downstairs. Interested?"

Elinor hesitated a moment. Knowing him would make it easier to find out about the letters. "I wouldn't mind meeting him," she said.

"He's very handsome, of course, but Luke says he wouldn't recommend any of his friends go out with him. Too old for you, for one thing."

Going out with him was the last thing Elinor wanted, but she needed some excuse for wanting to meet him and said, "I don't mind mature men. He should be interesting to talk to."

"He's cute but, you know, a bit fast."

"When Luke said that, he was probably just afraid you'd fall for him."

Gillie smiled contentedly. "He did seem a bit jealous when I was having coffee with Tony just now. Anyway, we'll have to make it snappy. He was in the cafeteria talking to the program director when I left."

Elinor took off her makeup gown and they went downstairs to the cafeteria. Tony Gower was still there, smiling and making himself agreeable to the station manager and program director, both men. He didn't look like a dangerous womanizer. Elinor noticed, though, that his head turned automatically when she and Gillie entered, and his eyes kept straying in their direction.

He was quite a bit older than Patrick, about thirty-eight or -nine. He was still attractive in a mature way. His face had a slightly worried look. His dark hair, silvering around the temples, gave him an air of authority. Only his blue eyes betrayed his rampant interest in women.

Before long, he left the men and came smiling up to Gillie. "Miss Parson," he said. "How nice to see you again." Elinor thought that he must have had professional voice training. His voice was mellifluous, as though his throat was lined with cream.

"Hi, Tony." Gillie smiled. "This is my friend Elinor Waring. We just popped down for a quick coffee. She's taping a spot this morning for tomorrow's show."

His smile was more wolfish now. It held a definite air of satisfaction—or anticipation. Elinor felt in her bones he was interested in her, not Gillie. She didn't believe for a moment that it was just her personal charms that appealed to him. Those glinting, predatory eyes were examining her to see how he could put her to use against Patrick.

"What a shame to waste all that beauty on children," he smiled. "I believe I saw you at the hotel yesterday, didn't I, Miss Waring?"

"Yes, I do the plants there."

He didn't mention her being with Patrick, but she was sure it was in his mind. "Will the taping session last long?" he asked.

"Only a quarter of an hour," Gillie said.

Gower's face wore a cunning look. He smiled blandly, but again his eyes gave him away. "I have to take a quick run down to the newspaper, but I'll be passing the station again in fifteen minutes. Why don't I come back and you ladies can join me for coffee?"

"I have to do the rest of my show while the audience is here," Gillie said. "We have six kids on the show each day."

"And you, Miss Waring? Do you have to dash off, too?"

Elinor smiled brightly. "Not at all. I'd like to meet you for coffee, Mr. Gower."

"Call me Tony, please! Break a leg, as they say in show biz."

He left, and Gillie grinned. "As easy as falling off a log, but I don't suggest you get serious about the guy."

"Don't worry. I'm not a masochist."

They went to the studio and Elinor did her presentation. She had been so busy she didn't have much material ready on the Christmas cactus, so she threw in reminders that the children keep their Christmas trees watered and turn off the electric lights when they left the room.

When she returned to the cafeteria, Tony hadn't arrived yet, which suited her just fine. It gave her a few minutes to think and to invent a plan for recovering the letters. She had decided he had them. Maybe this was the lead Jane Eliot had, too. If it was, Elinor meant to beat her and Patrick to the letters. And if it wasn't, so much the better. It would give her infinite satisfaction to hand them to Patrick and let him see she was just as wide-awake as Jane Eliot.

The letters, presumably, were in Tony's hotel room. Although it was about the last place she wanted to be, she didn't think it would be too difficult to lure him there. Getting out unmolested would be another matter. It would be easier and more logical to determine when he'd be out for an hour or so and get into his room by herself.

When he came hastening to her table a few minutes later, Elinor batted her eyes at him and smiled. "Tony, I was afraid you'd forgotten all about me," she said.

"I never forget a beautiful young lady," he replied with an answering smile. "Coffee?"

"To tell the truth, I've had two cups already today. It makes me jumpy. I'll pass, thanks."

"I don't need any more caffeine, either. We'll just chat and become a little acquainted. I've seen you more than once before," he said. His voice was turning smooth again, and his eyes began a blatantly admiring examination of her. "The first time was at the chamber of commerce ball, I think. Yes, you were wearing an extremely elegant dark blue gown. I wanted to dance with you, but you were taken."

She furrowed her brow a moment and said, "Oh, yes, I was with an old friend." Then she exclaimed, as if surprised, "You probably know the man I was with. Patrick Barron—he's with Congressman Firth's party, too."

"Of course, Patrick. You were having a word with him at the hotel yesterday, now that I think of it. Is he a good friend of yours, Elinor?"

She hesitated a moment, as though considering her answer. "An *old* friend," she answered.

"Lucky Barron."

Elinor glanced up at him provocatively from lowered eyelashes. "Since you know him, you could have asked for an introduction at the ball, couldn't you?"

"From the way he was looking at you, I didn't think he'd appreciate an interruption." There was a question in his eyes.

Elinor decided that he was digging to see if she said anything indiscreet. "There's nothing between us now. We used to go out years ago. I think he's seeing someone else these days."

Tony reached for her hands and squeezed them. "I can only say he has very poor taste. Whoever she is, she can't be as beautiful as you. Do you happen to know who the woman is?" he added nonchalantly, but the interest was still there.

Caught off guard, Elinor said, "A reporter, I think."

He nodded. "That would be Jane Eliot. She has a crush on him. They're pretty close. Were you and Patrick very... close?" he asked.

Elinor noticed that Jane Eliot was the first name that had popped into Gower's mind. She also wondered if he was angling to discover something to Patrick's discredit. "We used to talk about marriage," she said guardedly.

"What happened?" He was all ears.

"Careers got in the way," she said, shaking her head sadly. It was time to start executing her plan. She smiled flirtatiously. "You politicians are so busy. I know Patrick hasn't a minute to spare. Even though we're both in the same town again, he can't find time to call me. I imagine you're very busy, too, Tony." It was an invitation for him to respond and let her know when his room would be vacant.

"That's true," he said. "In fact, I'm playing hooky from a meeting right now. I really must dash back to the hotel. But perhaps we could meet later this evening."

It would be possible to search his room that morning while Gower was in the hotel, but Elinor preferred to do it when he was at some other spot entirely. "What about this afternoon?" she asked.

"I'm afraid I'm busy. I'll be briefing Congressman Firth on some background material regarding the economy. He's having a debate on television tonight with some members from the banking committee that's meeting here. I'll be with him for the debate, but it should be over by nine. We'll have a social hour with the bankers. I could meet you at ten." He looked for her answer.

The afternoon briefing would probably be done at the hotel. But while he was at the TV station for the evening debate, it would be a good time to search. The fact that Patrick would probably also be at the debate made it even better. Elinor had no true desire to meet Gower, but she decided to make the date to allay any suspicion. She could always phone the hotel and cancel the date.

"That sounds great," she said.

"I'll pick you up at your place shortly after ten."

Elinor silently noted that he didn't ask where she lived, which strengthened her suspicion that he'd already been there. He was obviously eager to get into her apartment again, probably to see what else he could find to incriminate Patrick and to pick her brains, as well. She was still angry with Patrick, but as her congressman, he would be infinitely preferable to this scavenger.

She went back to her shop and spent a busy day. By four o'clock her nerves were tattered from waiting and mulling over Patrick's behavior and dreading the evening. Breaking into Gower's room was nearly as unpleasant as going out with him.

During a lull in business, she went into the back room to unpack some Christmas plants. Lifting out fifty pots and checking them for damage was fairly hard work, but she preferred working with the plants to waiting on customers. Her hands became soiled, and when she wiped a wisp of hair back from her forehead, she left a trail of mud behind.

She heard the bell on the door jangle. She had installed it before she hired an assistant, to alert her to a customer if she was in the back. She didn't pay any attention now because Clare would handle it. Elinor stood with a trailing Boston fern in her hands when Patrick ducked his head through the low door into the back room and entered quietly.

As he stopped a moment and looked at her, a soft smile curved his lips. This was the image of Elinor that he carried deep in his heart—so deep he had thought he'd lost it. But this visit brought it surging back up to bedevil him. She was half forest nymph, half earth mother and totally bewitching. The grimy streak on her forehead only made her more desirable. Elinor became aware of the shadow in the doorway and looked up. Their eyes met, and for a moment neither said anything.

Chapter Eight

Elinor broke the silence. "Hi, Patrick," she said, crushing down the wild start of joy.

"Your welcome is underwhelming," he said as he sauntered in, brushing his way past palms and fig trees and poinsettias. Now what had got her dander up? Why was she looking at him as if he were a worm?

"You managed to wiggle out from under Firth's thumb for a minute, did you?"

"And came wiggling straight to you," he said, trying to cajole her into humor.

"I'm flattered. Would you mind putting this on that table behind you?" She handed him the fern, which he put aside.

"I have an hour free before I have to go and prepare for tonight's rubber chicken," he said.

"A whole hour? My, my. What will you do with so much time?"

"I'd like to spend it with you."

She gave a mock smile of delight. "Shall we hop a jet to Paris? Or maybe a warmer climate at this time of year. Rio, perhaps?"

He damped down his anger. "In any case, let's not waste it arguing. Can you get away for a while?"

It always piqued her that he assumed he'd call the shots and she'd jump. "Is your chauffeured limo waiting?" she asked ironically.

"No, I thought we might go next door for a coffee."

She sent him a hard look. "Will we be alone?" she asked, Jane Eliot in mind.

He looked confused. "I certainly hope so. That's the whole point, isn't it?"

There was alone as in all alone, just the two of them, and there was alone as in a coffee shop, surrounded by a couple of dozen patrons. It was the latter unsatisfactory alone that he meant, but at least Jane Eliot wouldn't be there so they could talk privately. Soon they wouldn't even be able to do that. Patrick was leaving in a couple of days.

"All right, let's go," she said, and picked up her sheep-lined corduroy jacket.

Patrick stopped her and pulled out his handkerchief. When he leaned over to wipe the grime off her forehead, she felt a tingle of pleasure up her spine. That's all he had to do to start her wishing and dreaming. "You can take the girl out of the country, but it's hard to get the country off the girl," he joked, rubbing.

"It's good, honest dirt. Not the kind you politicians deal in."

Patrick stuffed his handkerchief back in his pocket and grinned. "Sure. And I, for one, don't blame it for sticking to you. I just wish I could join it."

Elinor smiled spontaneously at the image this called up, and on this happier note they went next door to the coffee shop.

Patrick noticed as they went in that he could hardly have chosen a less romantic spot for this brief rendezvous. It was packed with customers lined up for take-out coffee and talking to one another in loud voices while waiting for their orders. The shop was bright and clean and efficient. From the white Formica counter to the linoleum floor and benches along the wall, it was about as romantic as a supermarket. The only good thing about it was the smell. The rich aroma of coffee, mingled with the yeasty scent of fresh pastries, hung in the air.

He led her to a booth at the back. The high walls allowed them some privacy. They ordered coffee and settled in to talk.

"It's strange that so many people are ruining their dinner by having a doughnut or sandwich at this hour," Patrick said.

"This is the working class," she replied. "A sandwich or doughnut probably *is* their dinner."

Patrick didn't want to get into an argument, but he sensed some hostility in her tone. If she thought his black jacket evenings were pure pleasure, she was mistaken. "It probably beats the rubber chicken at that. Do you want a sandwich?"

"No, thanks. Did you have any luck with the letters?" Elinor had mixed feelings about her question. If he had succeeded, it saved her from her pending ordeal with Tony Gower. However, she still wanted very much to best him.

"It didn't pan out," he admitted.

"What happened? You mentioned Jane Eliot had an idea."

"One of the scandal sheets has a reporter here trying to rake up some muck. Jane came up with the idea that he might have gotten the letters. That's the kind of nonnews they deal in—innuendo, misinterpretation. Apparently he followed us after the ball and he let that information slip to Jane. He was trying to pump her for news. She thought he might have broken into your apartment, but it seems she was mistaken."

"The bright Ms. Eliot mistaken?" she asked, laughing inside. This was her chance. She had thought of sharing her lead with Patrick but decided to go it alone. He'd probably be at the TV station with Firth at the crucial moment anyway. "How do you know?"

"I ransacked his briefcase while she distracted him this morning, and we got into his room later. He doesn't have them. He's working up a story on one of the foreign bankers instead."

So he and Jane must have been together for a good part of the morning. If she'd agreed to see him earlier, she might have been the one ransacking the reporter's room. "That's too bad," she said.

"What was your lead? You mentioned you were on to something."

She had foreseen the question and had a story ready. It annoyed her that he'd waited so long to ask, and even now he didn't sound very interested. With a mischievous smile, she said, "I thought maybe Jane Eliot herself took them. Oh, I know you trust her, but she mentioned the possibility that someone had followed us after the ball. I don't see why she couldn't have done it herself. She seems to be sticking pretty close to you. She's probably trying to dig up some dirt."

Patrick gave a dismissing laugh. "I don't think so. Jane doesn't indulge in that sort of low gossip. She's a very responsible journalist."

"And so bright. Well, I'm sure she'll find the letters, Patrick. Were you at Firth's briefing for the debate this afternoon?"

Patrick lifted a brow and stared. "How did you know about that?"

Elinor felt a twinge of guilt. She wouldn't have known if Gower hadn't mentioned it. "Everybody knows there's going to be a TV debate between the politicians and the bankers tonight," she said. "It's been advertised for a couple of days."

"But how do you know about the briefing?" Why was she blushing? She was more interested in his doings than she liked to admit.

She shrugged her shoulders. "Elementary, my dear Barron. Our leaders are always briefed before a public debate, aren't they? They wouldn't want the voters to see them with their facts down."

"Nobody can carry all the necessary statistics in his head," he pointed out, seeming to accept her explanation.

"Will you be at the station tonight, too?" she asked.

"Firth wants me to be there, but the debate's over at nine. Are you free then?"

Elinor hesitated a moment. Patrick was willing to forgo the social hour after the debate to be with her. Firth probably wanted him there, but he didn't make a big deal of it or even mention it. She wanted to see Patrick but wasn't sure what might happen at the hotel. Her search could lead her on to some other place, looking for the letters. And she wanted very much to have those letters in her hand the next time they met. She probably would be free by nine, though. "Why don't you call me?" she suggested.

He examined her closely. She felt a needle of guilt as he studied her with his sharp eyes. "I can pick you up at the shop, if that—"

"No, I close at six."

"I thought maybe with the Christmas rush, you were open late."

"No, I'm not."

"So what's the problem? Do you have a date?" he persisted.

She didn't mind letting him think that. And in a way, she did have a date, although she didn't intend to keep it. "I can probably get out of it," she said.

His eyes glowed with pleasure. "Good. I don't like the idea of your having unbreakable dates with anyone but me."

"I guess for the few days you're in town..."

Patrick kept studying her. He realized now that he was going to lose this woman if he didn't stake his claim in no uncertain terms. Since he'd found Elinor again, he'd learned he really didn't want to risk losing her. She was one in a million, the only woman that he literally couldn't resist. In silks and fancy hairdo or in jeans and dirty face, he wanted her. It would be damned awkward with the campaign coming up, but he'd manage it somehow. His hands closed possessively over hers.

When he spoke, his voice was burred with emotion. "We're going to have a long heart-to-heart talk before I leave town, Ellie."

The eyes that lingered on her face warmed her like a caress. Her heart throbbed at his touch and the longing in his voice. "Yes."

"Maybe tonight. I'll have to explain the situation to Firth. The party will be choosing their candidate next week. I have to be highly visible till then, but there will be a break over the Christmas vacation."

"I thought you already had explained it to him," she said.

But Firth didn't know that his candidate was planning to interrupt the campaign schedule with, hopefully, an engagement, a marriage and a honeymoon.

Patrick didn't want to propose in this workaday setting. He wanted his proposal to be as perfect as his bride. "I mean that it's taking a little longer than I thought," he said evasively. "At any rate, it'll be settled by Christmas."

"I always spend Christmas at home. Maybe you could come to the farm," she said impulsively.

His smile softened in pleasure. "I'd like that, but it could only be for a day or so."

A day or so. The Christmas break had suddenly shrunk to approximately twenty-four hours. "Is that all the time you get off for Christmas?"

"Well, no, but I should see my own folks, too."

"Oh, yes, of course." It was some small relief that business wasn't the distraction. She liked that Patrick had strong feelings for his family.

"Maybe you could visit my family for New Year's. It's only a hundred miles from your parents' to Rochester," he suggested.

"That would be nice. I'd really like that, Patrick."

"It's odd we never got around to visiting each other's home before, isn't it? They're not that far apart really." He wondered about that. In retrospect it almost seemed that he and Ellie hadn't been as serious as they pretended. He glanced at his watch. "Time's flying. Is there someplace we could be alone for a few minutes?"

She knew he wanted to kiss her, and she wanted it, too. She looked toward the window and saw it had begun to snow. It was only four-thirty, but at that season and with the sky covered by lead-gray clouds, it seemed like evening already.

"Let's walk in the snow," she said, and added silently to herself, "like we used to." Patrick used to put his arm around her and pull her close against him to ward off the chill. The newly fallen snow had sparkled like diamonds underfoot. It had been like walking through fairyland. Sometimes, at the darker spaces between street lamps, he'd pull her into his arms to steal a kiss.

He shook his head and put a bill on the table. "I don't know whether you're a sadist or a masochist, wanting to subject us to pneumonia, but if you want to walk, walk it is."

They went out into the softly falling snow. "I suppose you want to do some window-shopping," he said, turning to walk along the main street.

"No, this way," she countered, and led him around the corner, where the traffic was much thinner. There was only one other woman out walking, and a few cars crawled carefully by. The street lamps, which turned on automatically when it was dark, were already glowing, and a piercingly cold wind whistled down the street.

Patrick noticed that the sidewalks hadn't been cleared. He hadn't bothered to put on any snow boots, and his feet were freezing. But Ellie had already needled him a few times about his luxurious life-style, and he didn't want her to think he was spoiled.

They huddled into their coats and began trudging through the snow. As though he was reading her wishes, Patrick put an arm around her and pulled her against him. An ember of pleasure was fanned to a glow by the remembered intimacy. She thought Patrick felt it, too.

Then he peered down and said, "I don't suppose there's a sled team available in this town?"

"The way you talk, you'd think we were in Alaska. Don't they have snow in Washington?"

"Yes, but they have the strange habit of clearing it from the sidewalks."

"Don't be such a wimp," she said, and bumped him with her hip.

He looked down, enchanted with the sight of Ellie laughing in pleasure, with the soft, wet flakes clinging to her hair and eyelashes. It brought back memories.

"We used to do this when we were students. Remember how cold it was in New York?" He shuddered.

Good, he remembered! With a flush of confidence, she said, "I liked that so much. You said when you think of me, you picture me with my plants. I picture you in the snow."

"With a red nose and running eyes, you mean?"

"No, like this. Walking in the snow."

"With you, I hope? It's beautiful. Look how the snow sparkles."

The woman pedestrian passed them, and ahead a long stretch of privacy loomed. Patrick looked up and down and then stopped. "We used to do this, too," he said softly, and pulled her into his arms.

She lifted her face for his kiss. The snow fell gently, wafting down across her face, feather light. Elinor didn't feel cold at all. She felt warm and secure in the circle of his arms. It felt like a haven, but a haven should be for always, and she could tell how involved Patrick felt. Would she see him only during fleeting Christmas visits, only to say goodbye until the campaign was over? The election wasn't till next November, which was nearly a year away. Anything could happen in a year—especially with a beautiful, bright reporter named Jane Eliot following the campaign.

Patrick's lips moved and he cradled her head in the palm of one hand. After a moment he lifted his head and just gazed at her intently, unsmiling. "You look good not only in mud. You look terrific in snow. I wonder how you'd look in Mother Nature's other color, green."

"As in grass, you mean? Grass skirt?"

"No, actually I meant a fig leaf, as in nude."

She shivered. "Now who's the sadist? You'd want to rob me of a coat in this weather?"

"You should complain. At least you're wearing boots. My feet are freezing."

She looked down and noticed he was wearing only leather shoes, and in snow up to his ankles.

"Oh, Patrick! You should have told me!"

He shook his head, laughing. "I'm a willing martyr to love."

"You'll be a dead martyr if you don't get back to the hotel and change."

"Isn't that part and parcel of being a martyr? All the best martyrs die for the cause."

They ran to the corner and hailed a cab to take Patrick to the hotel. She felt a twinge of guilt when Patrick hopped in. She noticed his trousers were sodden at the bottom, and his socks must be soaked, too. He rolled down the window. "I'll call you around nine tonight."

"All right. Be sure you get out of those wet clothes."

He scowled playfully. "I notice you never make an offer like that when we're together."

They waved, and the cab pulled away. Elinor stood on the curb, watching the car. She wore a pensive frown. It was stupid of her to try to bring back the past. The past was gone, over and done with. All she'd accomplished was to expose Patrick to a cold. He'd changed, or at least the circumstances of his life had changed dramatically. He was no longer the carefree student who used to walk through the snow, kicking it up, climbing any available snowbank, making snowballs.

But for a moment, when he kissed her, it felt as though they had recaptured the past. And it felt very good.

Chapter Nine

Elinor thought a good deal before going to Tony Gower's hotel room that evening. She dreaded it but convinced herself it had to be done. If Thornby hadn't taken those letters and the press hadn't stolen them, then no one else but Gower could have done the deed. It wasn't just determination to outshine Jane Eliot that urged her on. She really wanted to help Patrick. She wanted to see his eyes shine with admiration when she handed the letters over to him. They would make a great Christmas present.

Tony's room wasn't a place she'd like to be caught alone if he returned unexpectedly for any reason. Patrick was at the debate, so he couldn't help her. The likeliest person to go with her was Gillie, who was, after all, her best friend. She went across the hall and knocked on Gillie's door.

Elinor was glad to see Gillie wasn't dressed up for an evening out. Her hair was all askew, and she wore an old plaid shirt over her slacks. "Are you busy tonight?" Elinor asked.

"Come on in, I'm just wrapping Christmas presents. Did you ever try to wrap a four-foot teddy bear without a box?" She looked at Elinor's coat. "Are you going somewhere?"

"That depends," Elinor said, and told her the whole story.

Gillie blinked in astonishment. "Holy cow! Why didn't you tell me any of this stuff? So *that's* why you wanted to meet Gower. I knew that he was up to no good. A whole soap opera going on next door, and you don't tell your best friend. I'm hurt, Elinor."

"And I'm sorry, but it's a secret, because of Patrick's political ambitions. You're the only one I've told."

Gillie was on the defensive. "I can keep a secret! And anyway, I hardly think loving you would do his career any harm."

"I'm a little hurt at that myself," Elinor admitted, "but it seems reporters take bits out of context and twist them around."

"Lowlifes. All right, I'll help you. Just wait till Luke hears this. After it's all over, I mean. I don't usually keep secrets from him, but seeing that it's you—and really it's not *my* secret, it's yours. Okay, let's go. How are we going to get into Gower's room?"

"Very carefully," Elinor replied. "Delivering a plant worked last night."

"Maybe we'd better try something else."

"Got any ideas?" Elinor asked.

"Nope."

"Then I guess a plant it is. And I just hope the housekeeping staff are in a friendly mood. I'll take one of my plants from home, to save stopping at the shop."

Elinor ran back to her apartment and picked up a poinsettia that she had brought home for Christmas. The pretty paper wrapping on its pot was still intact. They went out to the van together, discussing the job ahead of them.

When they reached the hotel, Gillie said, "I'll see if I can discover Gower's room number. I have my ID from the station, so they'll think I'm after an interview. I bet Gower's left orders that all reporters are to be given the red-carpet treatment."

The simple ruse worked. In a few minutes, Gillie joined Elinor in the lobby, where she was waiting. "Sixth floor, room 614. I just flashed my card and said, 'Press for Mr. Gower.' I watched and the clerk buzzed room 614. Now what?"

"Now I go and try my wiles on the bellboys. This might be tricky. Floors six and seven won't be very busy when all the politicians are at that debate. It works best if the bellboy has his arms full, too. Then it looks normal for me to go with him. If I succeed, I'll take the service elevator and meet you at Gower's room. You better wait around a corner so the bellboy doesn't get suspicious."

"Just like TV," Gillie grinned, and went toward the elevator.

Elinor took the plant to the housekeeping quarters and had the good fortune to meet the same bellboy who had let her into Rosco Devine's room the night before.

"Me again, with my flowers." She smiled. She looked at the card as though checking the name and said, "For a Mr. Tony Gower."

The bellboy shook his head. "Who'd be dumb enough to send flowers to a guy? Who are they from?" he asked, reaching for them.

"A secret admirer, I guess. I didn't open the card." She held on to the plant, wondering how she was going to arrange to deliver it herself.

"Are you going to give it to me or wait till the leaves fall off?" he asked impatiently.

"I'd like to take it up myself."

"Why?" He wasn't suspicious, just curious.

"I want to unwrap it and make sure it looks nice."

"All right, come on."

Elinor had no choice but to go with him. Any thorough search would be impossible, but she could take a quick look around. They were just leaving when the switchboard called to the bellboy.

"That order of ham on rye and coffee is ready for 620, Arnie."

Arnie handed the plant back to Elinor. "You mind carrying this for me?"

"Glad to."

They went together up the service elevator. The bellboy sidled closer and said, "So are you doing anything Saturday night? I'm off."

"I'm afraid I have a date."

"Do you go with somebody?"

"Sort of." She smiled evasively.

"My girl broke up with me. It's tough, working nights."

"Yeah, it sure is."

"Life's tough, then you die," he said philosophically.

The door opened and they went down the hall. Elinor didn't see any sign of Gillie. The bellboy opened door 614 and she went in. "Make it snappy, huh? I'm supposed to see the door's locked when I leave."

"I won't be a minute."

As soon as Elinor was inside, Gillie came hurtling down the hall and joined her.

"Quick, hide," Elinor said. "I have to pretend I'm leaving, but I'll be right back. You let me in. Okay?"

"*Capisce*. Knock three times." Gillie ran into the bathroom and closed the door.

Elinor removed the paper from the poinsettia and set the plant on the dresser. The bellboy was back in two minutes, and she left with him.

"I think I'll take the main elevator. Closer to the lobby," she said.

"No tips on the flower, I guess?"

"That's right. Tough luck."

As soon as he left, Elinor darted back to Gower's room and gave three light taps. Gillie had already begun the search. "His briefcase isn't here. He must have it at the studio, but I searched his luggage," she said. "He wears leopard-skin bikini shorts." She held them up and giggled. "Sexy or what? There's nothing else interesting here but this little black book full of women's names." She flipped through it and laughed. "And occupations," she added. "Call girls from all different states. The man's a creep. Boy, this is enough to finish Gower. Look what he says about Tiger Lily from Buffalo."

Elinor gave a "Tsk" of disgust. "No letters?"

"No."

"I'll try his jacket pockets. Would you mind taking a look under the pillows and mattress?"

They made a quick, nervous search of the room and found nothing. "I'm sure he has the letters," Elinor said. "They must be in his briefcase."

Gillie gave her a doubtful look. "You have a date with him tonight. If he has the briefcase with him at the studio, he'll still have it when he calls on you."

"I suppose so, but I don't want to see him. I was going to leave a message that I couldn't meet him."

"Suit yourself," Gillie said. "I can't say I blame you. It's too bad you couldn't get the letters, though. Maybe Patrick could help you."

"Oh, Lord! I forgot! I have a date with Patrick tonight, too. He's calling at nine. I better get home."

Gillie stared. "You have *two* dates? That's not like you, Ellie, to be so disorganized."

"It never rains but it pours. Let's get out of here," Elinor said. A shiver ran up her spine when she remembered she was here illegally.

"Shouldn't we take the little black book, just in case?"

"In case Patrick needs some ammo to counterattack, you mean? I doubt if he'd use it."

"Luke says all politicians have the killer instinct."

"Patrick doesn't!" Or didn't used to.

When Elinor turned to take the poinsettia, Gillie slid the little black book in her pocket and took the wrapper from the wastebasket, and they left. In the elevator, Elinor put the paper back on to protect the flower from the cold air outside.

They went down to the van and drove home. "I think I have the solution," Gillie said. "Patrick's phoning at nine. Gower isn't calling till ten. Tell Patrick the letters are in Gower's briefcase and let him snatch them. Then you leave a message at the hotel that you can't meet Gower, and you go out with Patrick."

"Gillie, you're a genius! That's what I'll do. You can have the poinsettia as a reward. Don't drown it, okay?"

"Gee, thanks. I'll take it to work and put it on the set. Your poinsettia will be world famous—in Delta, I mean. All the kids will see it. I'll tell them it's a present from the Plant Lady. That's what they call you."

They were home by eight-thirty. Gillie handed the black book to her friend. "You don't play dirty enough, Ellie. Take this. I took it when you weren't looking. It might come in handy."

Elinor took it reluctantly. "Even if it doesn't," she said, "it'll put a crimp in Gower's so-called love life."

They went to their separate apartments. Elinor decided to dress up for this date and took pains with her preparations. She chose an emerald green wool dress, because Patrick had wondered how she'd look in green. It was actually one of her best colors. The deep tone complemented her chestnut hair and brought out

the stormy gray of her eyes. By nine she was ready and
sat by the phone, waiting for its ring.

At 9:10 she told herself Patrick had been delayed a
little. Maybe the debate ran overtime. She flicked on
the TV, but the debate was over, so that couldn't be
the problem. At 9:15 she wondered if he'd decided to
just drive over, instead of phoning. This didn't leave
her much time to phone Gower. But the cocktail party
was at the station, and he'd be there till nearly ten, so
there was still time.

At 9:20 the phone finally rang, and to her horror it
was Tony Gower. "Elinor," his marshmallow voice
said. "A little change of plans. Helen Gordon, the
station manager's wife, has invited a bunch of us over
to their place. We have to stroke the media, you know.
A dead bore, but you could help liven up the evening.
How about joining me there?" He gave her the address.

Elinor hastily considered her options. Patrick still
hadn't called. Maybe he wouldn't call at all. She didn't
mind meeting Gower at someone's house as much as
she minded meeting him alone. There would be all
kinds of people there. Probably even Luke Williams.
Maybe he'd invite Gillie. With that many accom-
plices, she should be able to find Gower's briefcase
and search it. She'd have to let Luke in on the business of the letters, but she trusted him. She'd explain
to Patrick later. He could hardly object when she had
recovered the letters.

All this flashed through her mind in seconds, and
before Tony noticed any pause, she said, "That
sounds fine, Tony. What time?"

"This do at the station is starting to break up already. I'll be there by ten. Wear something sexy," he added in a deep, breathy tone that sent goose bumps of revulsion shivering up her arms.

Elinor doubted that he'd find her green wool very sexy, but she had no intention of changing. She darted over to Gillie's apartment to talk it over with her. Gillie was on the phone with Luke. She hung up and said, "I'm going to a party at the station manager's house."

"So am I," Elinor replied, and outlined the latest development.

"Great, we can go together. Does Patrick know?"

"I'm waiting for him to call."

"Then you better get back to your place or you'll miss it."

Elinor went back. She heard the phone ringing from the hall and ran the last steps. The phone stopped ringing just before she reached it. It must have been Patrick. She tried calling the station, but it took her so long to get someone to understand what she wanted and agree to try to find Patrick that she finally hung up in disgust. She'd been on the phone for more than five minutes, which prevented Patrick from getting through to her. She'd just have to hope he'd call again before she had to leave. There was still nearly half an hour. He'd call again.

But he didn't. Elinor began to wonder if that other call *had* been from Patrick. Maybe he just forgot all about his promise. She kept Gillie waiting until after ten to leave, in case Patrick called. By that time, she was so frustrated she didn't want to speak to him anyway. She remembered Gower's little black book and hid it beneath the swaying fronds of the Madagascar dragon tree.

"We might as well go," she said stiffly. "Something must have come up to detain Patrick. Probably another meeting with Firth."

Chapter Ten

The Gordons lived in the finest residential area of town. Trees lined the boulevard, and the houses were set well back on large lawns. Christmas lights at doorways and windows shone a welcome in this festive season. "So this is where the Gordons live!" Gillie exclaimed, staring enviously at a red brick Georgian house with double doors and fanlight windows. "I'd love to have a house like this someday."

Inside it was equally impressive. The marble-floored hallway was larger than Elinor's living room. It held an eight-foot Christmas tree, trimmed all in pink. Open doors to the left showed her connecting rooms, filled with fine furnishings. Smoke and perfume and conversation filled the air, setting a party mood. Mrs. Gordon met them at the door and welcomed them graciously.

When they were inside, Elinor saw at a glance why Patrick hadn't called. He was there—with Jane Eliot. They were in a dark corner with their heads together, enjoying an engrossing conversation. He didn't even see her. He was too preoccupied with Jane. Elinor's insides felt scalded with anger. Her first instinctive reaction was to stalk over and give him a piece of her mind. Her second was to go out the door and never see him again.

Before she did either of these, Gillie nudged her elbow and said, "There's Tony. Put on your best smile."

He had seen her and was coming forward, hand out to greet her. Elinor realized this would be the best revenge of all on Patrick.

"Elinor, you took me at my word," he said, looking her up and down. "Very nice." He didn't say "sexy," but the glitter in his eyes suggested it.

Tony helped her off with her coat. He led her into the living room, with his arm looped possessively around her waist. "Now who would you like to meet?" he asked in his actor's voice that attracted a lot of attention. He introduced her to a few of Congressman Firth's group, but later she couldn't remember their names. Patrick had finally noticed her and sat like a frozen statue, glaring from his dark corner. Jane Eliot had her hand on his arm, as if restraining him.

Elinor tossed her head and smiled brightly up at Tony. "What do you say we get a drink, Tony? I'm parched."

He examined her closely. "We'll have a couple of quick ones, then cut out." The tremble of fear and revulsion crawling up her spine felt like the tread of a rat. Between that and her acute awareness of

Patrick's anger, she felt ready to burst. "What's your poison?" he asked.

Distracted, Elinor answered, "I'm not fussy. Eggnog, I guess, if they have it." She went off to the next room to wait, as she was afraid Patrick was preparing to make a scene. He kept staring at her, waiting for his chance to get her alone.

The drink Tony handed her tasted very strong. Under the plushy richness of the eggnog there was more than rum. She wondered if he'd spiked it with brandy or something. It burned her throat, so she sipped very slowly. She knew Tony's plan was to get her out of here, alone someplace, half-intoxicated if he could manage it. So she didn't have much time to get into his briefcase, and she didn't even know where it was.

Like a clever politician, Tony didn't waste all his time trying to seduce his date. He circulated through the crowd, talking to anyone who might help his career. At her first opportunity, Elinor went up to Luke and Gillie. "Did you talk to Patrick?" Gillie asked.

"No, it looks like there's going to be a change of plans," she said. "Patrick's busy. I'll handle this myself—with your help."

Elinor realized that Luke would be a good accomplice, and she outlined her plan. He urged caution.

"I wondered why you came with Gower," he said. "He's not the kind of guy you should be out with, Elinor. You should hear the way he talks about women."

"Luke drove Tony here," Gillie said. "Did he bring his briefcase, Luke?"

"Yes, he left it in the car. He particularly asked me to lock the car so no one could get at it. I wondered at

the time why he was carrying around critical docu-
ments."

Gillie winked over his shoulder. "He was probably
afraid somebody would get into his hotel room and
steal them."

"Nobody would be that foolhardy," Luke said.

The women exchanged conspiratorial glances.
"Handy that you have the car key," Gillie said.
"Didn't you leave something in your car, Luke?"

"My, uh, handkerchief? Yeah, that's it. I feel a cold
coming on." He ducked out of the room, and when
Gower wasn't looking he left the house.

Elinor returned to Tony. Happy that she was about
to ruin his plans, she even forced herself to put her
hand on his arm without shuddering. "Are you ready
for another drink?" he asked. She noticed the eagerness in his voice. She had hardly touched the eggnog.

"Not yet."

"Drink up, honey. We'll be leaving soon. I spotted
a stringer from *Time* magazine over by the punch
bowl. I'd like to have a word with him, but I'll be right
back."

"Do hurry." She smiled flirtatiously. He didn't even
bother trying to get to know her. She was just a convenient woman. If he had his way, her name would be
added to his little black book. She smiled inwardly to
think she had gotten that away from him. Any reluctance she felt to help Patrick was more than made up
for by the desire to thwart Tony Gower.

Elinor knew Luke couldn't be back from the car yet,
but she looked around for Gillie. She purposely kept
her eyes from the corner where Patrick and Jane Eliot sat together. She didn't see Patrick and she didn't

forget him, but when he came up behind her and touched her on the elbow, she was startled.

She turned and found herself staring into the angriest eyes she'd ever seen. His face was flushed, which accentuated the strained white patches around his lips and nose. "Just what the hell do you think you're doing?" he demanded in an icy voice.

She felt a thrill at being able to make him this furious. It lent a husky quality to her voice. She took a sip of her drink and answered with studied nonchalance, "Same as you. Enjoying a party with my date. Where's Jane? I must say hello to her."

"She's not my date. And that doesn't excuse you for going out with that sleaze Gower. You know what he's like."

She gave an infuriating smile. "I know he's very handsome, at any rate."

The muscles in his jaws quivered with the exertion of controlling his temper. "I'm taking you home." He put a hand on her arm.

She lifted it off as though it were a dirty rag. "I always go home with the man who brought me. If you had invited me, that'd be you, Patrick. But as you forgot to call..."

He broke impatiently into her speech. "I called you a dozen times! You weren't home."

"I stepped over to Gillie's for a minute," she admitted. "I see you were so anxious to party that you came on without me. You might have called once while I was out. Not a dozen times, I think."

"Well, twice, then. First the line was busy, then you were out—or did you and Gower decide to take the phone off the hook?"

"Now why would we do that?" A rage shook her as she realized what he was implying.

"You seem very thick with Gower all of a sudden." His flushed face turned suddenly white. It emphasized the dark, accusing anger of his eyes. "Or is it all of a sudden?" he demanded.

Elinor's voice was tense with fury. "If you're implying something, why not just come right out and say it?"

Patrick found his throat was paralyzed. It couldn't be—Ellie and Tony Gower? Had she given him the letters? My God, did she hate him that much? Jane had told him Elinor was seen with Tony at the TV station that morning, but he thought it had been an accidental meeting, though he wondered why she hadn't mentioned it. And he'd been wondering how she'd learned about the briefing session.

How could they have met? Tony would have been at pains to arrange it, of course, once he learned of her connection with Patrick. Probably he was the one who gave her the idea there was something between him and Jane Eliot. He was using Elinor, but why was she letting him? He remembered her few snide comments about politicians, but that was hardly enough to infuriate her. Apparently Gower had a way with women. He must have fed her some lie to turn her against Patrick.

"How long have you known him?" he demanded.

"I never met him before this convention."

"He works fast."

She gave him a scathing look. "Unlike some men, Tony always keeps his dates. That speeds things up."

He leaped on it. "Always? Then you *have* met him before!"

"I don't have to account to you for my friends."

"By God, you have to account to me for this one! You said you were helping *me*. Some help, stabbing me in the back. Don't think you'll get anywhere with Gower. He'll use you and throw you aside."

Her gray eyes were nearly black with anger. "That won't be a new experience for me! And how dare you imply I'm stabbing you in the back! I'm only with Tony because of you."

"I never asked you to go to these lengths."

"Do you want the letters or not? It's pretty hard to help someone who never shows up or calls when he's supposed to! I decided to do it by myself."

"I called you twice! I was going to ask you to meet me here."

"You weren't near a phone when I got here. You were in a corner snuggling up with Jane Eliot. Go on back to her, Patrick. She can do your career a lot more good than I can. But just be careful you don't write her any love letters. You can see what a pain in the neck they'll become when you're ready to drop her."

"Jane is just a friend, whatever Gower told you. She's helping me find the letters. You know that."

She gave a superior little smile. "You and Jane can relax. I've taken care of the letters."

"You've got them?" His brows drew together as he tried to fit this in with his theory that she was helping Gower. It didn't jibe.

"Of course, I don't claim to be as bright and wide-awake as Jane, but at least I figured out who'd want them, besides Harry Thornby."

"Where are they?"

"Details at eleven," she said, and walked away.

It was an exultant moment, to show Patrick she was just as clever as his precious Jane Eliot. She was glad to see he was jealous, too—or angry, at least. A quick peek into the next room showed her that Tony was still busy with the stringer from *Time*, so she walked into the hallway to wait for Luke's return. Within thirty seconds, Patrick followed her. They were alone in the spacious hall. His tense posture was the only evidence of his mood.

"Don't try to walk away from this, Elinor. I want to know how you got those letters."

She turned on him in fury. "What difference does that make? All you wanted was the letters. Well, you'll get them, don't worry. You'll get your precious letters. And I can assure you it wasn't necessary for you to pretend you still loved me to do it."

"I don't recall using the word love!"

"You're right. I noticed you were careful to avoid it. You should do well in politics, Patrick. You've learned all the tricks, to imply what you don't mean, in order to manipulate people. When I think what I went through to get the letters back . . . Maybe it was worth it to find out what you're really like."

They heard some commotion on the stairway and stopped arguing. Two women came down, smiling and talking. One of them recognized Patrick and spoke to him. Elinor took the opportunity to leave. As soon as Patrick went back into the living room, she returned to the hallway to wait for Luke. He came back in a few minutes.

"Any luck?" she asked.

"They weren't there," he answered.

"They have to be!"

"They're not in his briefcase. They must be at the hotel."

"They're not. We looked."

He pinned her with a brilliant blue eye. "We? You mean you and Barron?"

She gulped. "Ask Gillie," she said, and went off to warn her friend of the slip. She didn't realize Gillie hadn't told Luke about the hotel escapade.

"Oh, brother! Luke'll hit the roof. I didn't tell him that," Gillie said. "Never mind, I can handle Luke. What are you going to do now?"

"I'd just like to go home and bury myself under six inches of blankets."

"That might not be a bad idea. Why don't you go, Elinor? And I'll tell Gower you felt sick."

"Okay, I will. He'll think it was the brandy he spiked my eggnog with. Thanks for everything, Gillie. I'm sorry if I caused you any trouble with Luke."

"Forget it. He doesn't own me—yet. What will I tell Patrick?"

"Nothing. He doesn't own me, either."

Elinor slipped quietly away from the party and was relieved to breathe in the fresh, cold air. It felt so clean after being with Tony Gower. She drove home slowly, thinking about where the letters could be. Rosco didn't have them, and Patrick had thought he was the likeliest person from the opposition side to have taken them.

But Gower didn't have them, either. Maybe he'd already given them to Firth? But Patrick had told Firth about the letters. For that matter, would Gower show them to Firth? It would look pretty spiteful to be gathering evidence against his own competitor. She thought Tony would be more subtle than that. If she were Gower and she did have the letters, she wouldn't show them to Firth. But she'd want to make them public knowledge, so she'd contact someone from the press. She'd give them to a sleazy reporter, but Jane wasn't sleazy.

Gower wasn't after money, or he'd have approached Patrick. Maybe the opposition party would be willing to pay him for them. Rosco seemed to be the man in charge of dirty tricks for Thornby. Were Gower and Rosco working as a team? This felt sneaky enough to be right.

She went home and locked the door behind her. Then she checked to see that the little black book was still hidden under the Madagascar dragon tree. It was there. She left it where it was and went to the sofa to think.

At the party, Jane Eliot said to Patrick, "You look as if someone had knocked the wind out of you. What happened?"

"I don't know. I can't fit the pieces of this puzzle together, Jane. Nothing adds up. Elinor being here with Gower."

"She just sneaked out the door alone. She was probably trying to help you. You should warn her against Gower. He plays rough."

"She knows what he's like. Very well," he said bitterly.

"If you're thinking what I think you're thinking, forget it. She didn't give Gower the letters. You know she didn't even meet him till this morning, and the letters have been missing longer than that."

"I *don't* know. She said she got the letters back. How did she work that miracle?"

Jane squirmed. "I only know one thing that might possibly work with a guy like Gower. And I don't think your Elinor would oblige him."

Patrick leaped up. "Good God! She wouldn't!" Terrible images swarmed through his head. He felt in his bones that Elinor was too sweet and innocent to purposely harm his career. But if she'd given herself to Gower to get those letters back, he'd never forgive any of them. She had sounded so anguished when she'd said those words: "What I went through to get the letters back . . ."

"I've got to see her."

He ran from the house without remembering to pick up his coat or call a taxi. The wind whipped around him as he hurried to the main street to hail a cab. The cold stabbed like a knife, but he didn't notice it. He was fevered with anxiety and regret.

Chapter Eleven

Elinor's thoughts went back to the party and were soon harping on the short meeting with Patrick. She had been too agitated before to mull over all the implications of their conversation, but now it all came back. "You seem very thick with Gower." "How long have you known him?" "He works fast." And worst of all, "Or did you take the phone off the hook?" That one really cut deep. He'd been implying that she was having an affair with Tony. "Stabbing me in the back" even suggested that she was helping Tony. Surely he knew her better than that. Couldn't he figure out why she was subjecting herself to that lecher's company?

While Elinor sat thinking, there was a sudden pounding at the door. She jumped up from the sofa in alarm. The first awful thing that came to her mind was that Tony had shown up. She sat perfectly still, hoping her visitor would go away. The banging came again, louder now, bolder, more insistent.

"Ellie, are you there? Let me in, it's Patrick."

Patrick! The rhythm of her heartbeat changed from fear to anger, but inexplicably tinged with joy. At least she wasn't physically afraid of him, though she wasn't sure she wanted to see him, either.

The hammering grew louder. She got up and called, "What do you want?"

"I have to see you."

His voice sounded strangely tense. She decided to let him in. When she opened the door she was confronted with a different expression than she expected. She knew Patrick was angry. She was livid with fury herself, but the sight of him made her forget everything else. He looked almost gray, wounded, drained of life. Even his eyes seemed glazed with moisture.

"What's the matter? Are you hurt?" she exclaimed.

He didn't answer. He just looked at her in a strange, heart-wrenching way. She helped him into the living room, checking discreetly for signs of injury. Where was his coat? He was freezing cold.

"Patrick, what's the matter?" she repeated, her voice rising in anxiety.

He found he couldn't answer her. Even if he could have found words to say, his throat was too clogged to speak them. He just pulled her into his arms and clung to her as if his life depended on it. Ellie looked so sweet and worried. All the love she occasionally tried to hide was shining in her eyes. Her love had led her to barter herself to that fiend Gower to help him. It was all his fault, and he felt sick with guilt and remorse.

Even through her wool dress, Elinor felt the awful cold emanating from him. He was trembling with it, but when he spoke, his voice was hot. He didn't look at her. He just spoke into her ear in a strange, choking whisper.

"I'm quitting politics, Ellie," he said. "It isn't worth it. It just isn't worth it. I'm sorry, darling. I know you did it for me. I'll never forgive myself. The letters weren't that important."

He sounded so distracted that Elinor thought he must be intoxicated. She led him to the sofa. "Sit down, Patrick. I think I should make some maté. That'll calm you."

He slumped down, covered the bottom of his face with one hand and murmured, "Thanks. That will help." It would give him a minute to collect his thoughts, but he never wanted to think again. He just wanted to wipe the knowledge and memory of Elinor's sacrifice from his mind forever. He wanted to start their lives, or at least this reunion, all over again.

Elinor thought the desperate eyes glowing at her looked as if they needed a stronger restorative than maté. She hurried to the kitchen and came back as soon as the kettle was on. Patrick took her hand and kissed it, then held it tightly. His face felt warm now. His hand felt quite hot.

"Was it awful?" he asked softly, gazing at her from his troubled, dark eyes. Then he shook his head. "No, don't tell me. I can't bear to hear the details."

She couldn't make any sense of it but tried. "Was what awful? Being with Tony?"

"Yes, being with Tony."

"It was bad enough. I guess the brandy in my drink was the worst part of it. I think he was trying to get me tight."

His words came out in a bark. "The creep, I'll kill him."

He jumped up, and she pulled him back down. "Relax. I only took a few sips."

"Then you were sober when it—happened?"

He was either drunk or insane. "When what happened?"

He cleared his throat, unable to say the words. As long as he didn't say it, it could remain amorphous. A nameless tragedy. She waited, and he finally muttered, "The letters—when did you get them?"

She drew a deep sigh. "I didn't. I thought I had them, but he outwitted me. First I thought they were in his hotel room, but I couldn't find them. They weren't in his briefcase, either."

Patrick clenched his jaws at that casual "in his hotel room" and asked, "How many times were you out with him?"

"Just once. Tonight."

"But he was at the debate. You couldn't have—" He looked at her, hope dawning as he rapidly considered the evening's events.

"I met him at the TV station this morning. He asked me out and I accepted, but I didn't really intend to go till you..."

"I called," he reminded her. "I was even calling again when you came into the party and Gower was waiting for you. I'd heard him bragging about his date and knew it was prearranged, although he didn't mention his date's name. He was at the debate. He went straight from the station to the party. He didn't have time to meet you at the hotel."

She gave him a blank look. "You don't think I'm stupid enough to go into a hotel room with a creep like that! I knew he'd be at the debate and took advantage of it to search his room. Gillie and I sneaked in while he was away."

Patrick was so overwhelmed with gratitude to fate that for a moment no words came. He cleared his throat and said, "I think you'd better tell me this story from the beginning."

"The water's boiling. I'll make tea first."

Elinor went to the kitchen, pondering this bizarre visit and Patrick's devastated condition. What had he meant by asking her if it had been awful? And then he'd said he couldn't bear to hear the details. He hadn't been talking about her efforts to get the letters, unless he'd thought she'd—Good Lord, was *that* it? The fear that she had seduced, or been seduced by, Gower left Patrick limp. A slow smile spread across her lips. He'd even promised to give up politics. If that wasn't love!

In the living room, Patrick leaned back, wondering if he was dreaming. It was all right. Gower hadn't got at her. Patrick wouldn't have to kill him after all. Ellie was safe. A feeling of peace and joy swelled in him. How soft and moist and beautiful the air was in here, with the plants stirring in the current from the humidifier. He breathed in deeply. It felt like paradise. His throat, unfortunately, felt like sandpaper. He was coming down with a king-size case of flu.

Elinor wore a mysterious smile when she returned with the tea tray. "You know, since you've decided to give up politics, I guess the letters really don't matter anymore. Have you thought what you'll do for a job, Patrick?"

He looked at her warily. "I did say that, didn't I?"

"Yes, you did. With your law degree, you could always go into private practice."

He answered uncertainly. "It'd seem pretty dull after politics."

"Peaceful," she countered. "And so much less time-consuming."

"Yes."

She poured the steaming tea into his cup. "This reminds me of you," she said.

"My grandmother got me hooked on maté."

She slid a glance at him. "I didn't mean the maté. I just meant the hot water, which you always seem to be getting yourself into lately. Don't worry, I won't hold you to that rash promise to quit politics. Actually it wasn't a promise. You avoided the important word—again. I don't think you should quit. They say people get the politicians they deserve. If men like you quit, it'll leave the field wide open for the other sort—like Gower."

"I would quit, if I thought anything like I imagined tonight would ever happen to you. I thought—"

"I know what you thought. Thanks for the vote of confidence. I'd give you hell, if your reaction hadn't been so flattering."

He shook his head. "I felt like scum. Lower than scum. Like a slug or some blight that had killed a beautiful blossom. *Promise me* you'll never do anything like that, Ellie."

He reached for her hand. She picked up the teacup and tossed her shoulders impertinently, but there was a warm glow of pleasure inside. He had really meant it, that he'd quit his beloved politics when he thought she had—it was too gross to think of.

"Don't flatter yourself," she said. "I have my standards, and not even helping out in a good cause would permit me to do that. Now, about the letters..."

"To hell with the letters. Let him make what he can of Plato."

"Plato? What's he got to do with it?"

"I told you, I was reading Plato's *Republic* the summer I wrote them. All that misguided philosophy about democracy resulting in tyranny. Plato's favored regime was what he called communism, you know. His communism has very little to do with the current sort. The word has taken on different associations since the third century B.C. But it wouldn't do my reputation any good to be branded as a communist."

Elinor listened, disbelieving. "What are you talking about? They were love letters."

"Yes, and they were also reports about what I was doing and reading. Don't you remember?"

She remembered that some parts of the letters were less interesting to her than others, and it was the more interesting parts she had reread a dozen times. "Is that what all this was about—Plato?"

"No! I didn't particularly want the world to read the more personal bits, either. They were written to you alone. If your eyes happen to remind me of the stormy Atlantic, that's our business."

It was too absurd. Elinor felt like laughing, yet as she considered it, she realized Patrick was right. The love passages would only amuse and titillate; the other parts could be more damaging—very damaging. "I wouldn't dismiss the letters at this point," she cautioned.

"Trying to find them has been nothing but trouble. You thought I was chasing Jane. I thought you were seducing Gower." He gave her a rakish smile. "It didn't leave us a minute to seduce each other. We've looked all over hell's half acre, and can't find them."

"I think I know where they are, though," she said, and watched as his interest grew.

"Where?"

"Unless Gower has already given them to Rosco, they're probably in the hotel vault."

"Rosco! That's a possibility." He considered it a moment. "Of course that's what he'd do with them. Gower wouldn't dare risk leaking them to the press himself. It'd reveal that he puts his own good above the party, and that's a no-no. And he wouldn't openly flout party unity by taking them to Firth. That's the main reason I didn't believe he had taken them. Firth is always stressing the importance of party unity. The good of the party comes before personal good. But if Gower could get the opposition to leak them, he'd keep his nose clean. You're smarter than Jane and me put together."

She blew on her nails and polished them on her dress. "Just because I'm a small-town girl, it doesn't mean I can't add two and two. Even if I do occasionally get five," she added, with a thought of Jane.

"All right, wizard, help me figure out how to get them out of the hotel safe. I imagine that's where they are. I haven't noticed Rosco leering at me, at least. He'd be showing signs of joy if he had them. I don't suppose you happen to have a blowtorch?"

"It can't be done. We'll have to have Gower get them out for us."

"That, of course, will be a snap."

"Yeah," she said, and laughed.

Patrick looked alarmed. "Ellie! Don't even *think* it. You're not going to see him again. I forbid it!"

"You don't own me! Oh, I'd love to see his face when I tell him I have his little black book."

Patrick stared in disbelief. "You're kidding! You've got his little black book?"

"I nabbed it when I was searching his hotel room with Gillie. I figured it might come in handy. You wouldn't *believe* what he does with Tiger Lily, Patrick."

"Good Lord." He put his head back and laughed till the tears ran down his face. "And I was worried about a mere accusation of being a communist. There's got to be enough scandal in that book to sink Gower for all eternity. Where is it?"

"In the pot by the window, if it hasn't self-ignited. It's pretty hot."

"The hotter, the better." He gave a shiver. "It's cold in here, though, isn't it?"

"The thermostat says seventy-two degrees. Are you feeling chilly?" He shivered again and rubbed his throat. "You must have caught a chill, going out without a coat tonight."

"I think it was that romp through the snowbank without boots this afternoon that did it. I've been feeling a bit uncomfortable all evening."

"Sure, blame me," she said, but she did feel guilty and got a blanket to put over his shoulders before retrieving the book. "Tony's going to be wondering what happened to me," she mentioned. "I told Luke to tell him I felt ill. If he's a gentleman—foolish thought—he'll call and see if I got home all right."

"He uses the manners of a gentleman. It's the morals that are lacking. I imagine he'll call."

"Want to stick around for the swap?" she asked.

Patrick shivered again and said, "You'd better let me handle it."

She gave him a knowing look. "With the same skill and finesse and lack of success you've handled it with up till now? No thanks, but you can stick around for moral support if you like. We'll just wait a while, shall we, and see if he phones? I wish I had a fireplace, but since I don't, I'll turn on the Christmas tree lights. They *look* warm, at least."

"You might as well turn off the lamps, then," Patrick suggested. "The colored lights are prettier in the dark."

She plugged in the string of lights and lowered the lamps. They sat together in the shadows on the sofa, looking at the tree. Patrick looked so cozy in his blanket. She thought he might suggest that they both bundle up in it, but he just pulled it more tightly around his shoulders and said, "If he doesn't call before he gets back to the hotel, he'll call soon after."

"Yes, as soon as he sees his little black book is missing. I imagine he'll suspect us."

Patrick opened the book and began glancing at some of the entries. "What does it say?" she asked, moving closer.

He moved farther down the sofa. "I can't see much. It's too dark, but it wouldn't be fit for a young lady's eyes."

"Then it isn't fit for Caesar's wife," she replied, and made a lunge for it.

Patrick grabbed her wrist, and she tumbled against him. The blanket fell open, and she felt her breasts yielding against the wall of his chest. Her head was caught against his shoulder, in the curve of his upper arm. Their eyes met, just inches apart. She put her hand on his shoulder to prevent falling into his lap. All he had to do was move her hand....

She smiled an invitation. His lips quivered a moment, then firmed. The air felt still, and in the corner, the Christmas lights twinkled, adding an air of enchantment. The whole scene reeked of romance, and Elinor waited with bated breath for him to make a move.

"Need a hand?" he asked, and gently pushed her away.

She sat up, straightening her dress and feeling like a fool. "I could call Tony," she said, trying to sound casual. "We don't want to be stuck here all night." Although she spoke calmly, she felt stung that he had rejected her.

"We'll give him till eleven-thirty."

"Right. We can't wait all night. I'd like to get to bed for a few hours. The shop'll be busy tomorrow."

"It's doing well, is it?"

Elinor was grateful for this line of conversation, since it tended to smooth over the embarrassing moment. "Terrific, especially around Christmastime."

"And you have an acre of greenhouse on the farm, I think you said?"

"Yes. I plan to expand to two."

"That must have cost you a lot."

"I got a loan from the bank. It's paid off now," she said.

"The other woman in your shop—Clare, is it?"

"Yes."

"Is she a partner or..."

"No, just a clerk. I own the whole thing, lock, stock and barrel."

"Funny expression—lock, stock and barrel. Sounds as if it might refer to an old general store. Lock on the door, stock of supplies and the barrels the men used to sit on, smoking."

"I always thought it had something to do with guns."

This rambling talk sounded to Elinor as if Patrick was trying desperately to avoid any more personal conversation. He was already regretting that spontaneous outburst about quitting politics. It just meant too much to him. He didn't have time for her. He was probably wondering how he could get out of visiting her for Christmas. She decided to test him.

"About that Christmas visit we discussed..."

He coughed into the blanket. "I wouldn't want to take this cold home to your family. Some Christmas present."

"Yeah, some present. Maybe we'd better just forget it."

He nodded. "That might be best. But you'll visit me for New Year's? I should be better by then."

"Actually, that's a busy time for me, too. All those corsages for the New Year's balls."

Before he could answer, the phone rang. Elinor jumped up. "I'll get it. That could be Tony."

"Do you have an extension? I'd love to hear this."

"No." She picked up the receiver. "Hello, Elinor Waring here." Patrick got up and stood close, trying to hear.

"Elinor, it's Tony. Are you all right, dear?"

"Actually, I'm feeling quite nauseated, Tony. It's either the brandy you slipped in my drink or this little black book I've been glancing at. It's enough to make anyone sick."

"What—what do you mean, Elinor?" His voice sounded wary.

"I think you know what I mean. The book has your name on it. That wasn't very discreet of you."

An explosion of profanities poured into her ear. She held the phone away in disgust. Patrick took it with a gleeful grin. "Same to you, buddy, in spades. Are you ready for a swap?" he asked.

"How did you know I have the letters?"

Patrick winked at Elinor. "I have a very bright accomplice. How long will it take you to get the letters?"

"I can be there in half an hour."

"We'll meet at the hotel. I don't think the young lady is eager to dirty her apartment with trash. Half an hour, in your room at the hotel." He hung up the phone and lifted Elinor's arm in a symbol of victory, laughing. The blanket fell to the floor.

"We did it. No, *you* did it. How can I ever thank you, darling?" He kissed her lightly on the cheek, then pulled her into his arms, but he didn't give her a real kiss. He just hugged her violently. "I better call a cab."

"I'll drive you," she offered.

"No way. That means you'd have to drive home alone. Not that I don't trust you!" he added with a laughing look. "It's the men I don't trust."

And by taking a taxi, he didn't have to see her again. "Let me know how it turns out," she said coolly.

"I'll call you from the hotel. I'd come back, but with this cold coming on, I think bed is the place for me."

"I'll call the cab," Elinor said in a dull voice.

It arrived with unnecessary speed. Patrick tucked the little black book into his pocket and left, without even kissing her goodbye. "I'll call you later. Don't leave the phone off the hook, huh?"

"I'll be waiting," she said, and even managed a smile. She got the door safely closed before the tears came.

Chapter Twelve

Elinor's plants were her favorite company when she was sad. They didn't try to cheer her up by saying it was probably for the best. They didn't offer the absurd fiction that there were better fish in the sea than the one that got away. She knew there wasn't a better one than Patrick for her; the one you loved and wanted was the best one. The plants just sat there passively, demanding her attention without jarring her emotions. She pampered them awhile, trying to distract her thoughts from the bleak future.

Gillie's fern was looking better already. She'd caught it in time, before the roots rotted. The draft blowing in around the kitchen windowsill told her this was a bad place for the sensitive fern, so she moved it in among the window plants in her living room and resisted the temptation to water it. Only the topsoil was dry. It would still be sodden below.

This routine work allowed Elinor's thoughts to stray, and mainly they strayed to Patrick. She should have tried harder to keep him. But a busy congressman needed a wife who could conduct herself in high society. Mrs. Barron would be expected to have large dinner parties. She'd have to entertain important people, and she'd have to know a lot more about politics than Elinor knew. Patrick was so serious about his career that he should marry that kind of woman.

It was three-quarters of an hour before he called from the hotel, but it hadn't seemed very long at all. At 12:15 the eerie silence of the apartment was shattered by the ring of the phone. "Mission accomplished," he said. "I've got the letters."

"What did Gower say?"

"He suggested nasty, brutish and physically impossible things I should do to myself. Things that I prefer not to go into with you in any detail. If I'd been carrying a hidden tape recorder, the tape would have self-destructed on the spot. Fortunately, my ears are stronger. Quite apart from my own self-interest in all this, I'm really glad Gower's career is torpedoed. The people deserve better than that."

"It didn't come to blows?" she asked.

"Not physical ones. We battered each other with some rather strong name-calling. I'll tell Firth tomorrow morning that I have the letters. Don't be surprised if you read in the papers soon that I've got the party's nomination for their candidate." His voice lowered to a more intimate tone. "Thanks, Ellie. You're the one who did it."

"That's fair. You wouldn't have had to worry about the letters if you hadn't written them to me in the first place."

His voice took on a sultry tone. "All your fault in a way. If you weren't so beautiful—"

He had a little coughing fit, and Elinor said, "If I weren't so beautiful, you wouldn't have been quoting Plato, you mean? What did you do with the infamous letters? Did you burn them?"

"Not yet," he said rather reluctantly. "I was just looking them over. I want to read them thoroughly before I do. They bring back fond memories. They were good times, weren't they, Ellie?"

"Yes, they were," she said softly. They certainly had been good times—the best—but she feared that past tense pretty well summed it up. She mentally squared her shoulders and asked, "When will you be leaving Delta?"

"You sound eager to be rid of me."

In a way she was. The sooner he packed up and left, the sooner her life could return to normal. There was no point in dragging out the painful inevitable. "The bankers' convention is over. All the reporters will be rushing off. I don't imagine you politicians will stick around, looking for coverage in the *Delta Daily Journal.*"

"Firth's staying home for Christmas. He invited me, but of course I don't intend to land an invalid in on his family. He's lending me the limo and Ron for the trip home."

"That'll impress them in Rochester. It sounds like you're the heir apparent, all right."

"It won't be official till the party gives it their okay, but between us, the deal is settled. The reason he's lending me the car is because of my delicate condition." He coughed again. "Do I sound like Camille?"

"More like a bullfrog. You better get to bed, Patrick, but before you go, I want to wish you a Merry Christmas."

"It won't be that merry without you, but we have New Year's to look forward to. Good night, darling. And thanks for everything."

It was probably just his sore throat that caused that hoarse rumble in his voice. "Always glad to help," she said.

"I hope that's a promise. I mean to hold you to it." He gave a little laugh and hung up.

Before she went to bed, Elinor took the silver-framed picture of Patrick from her bottom drawer and looked at it for a long time. As her eyes traced the familiar outline of hair and eyes and mouth, her mind roved over the past with fond remembrance. The frame had tarnished to brown. What pleasure she used to take from polishing it.

She didn't have any silver polish but cleaned it with toothpaste, then cleaned the glass. The picture looked like new again, the way it had when he gave it to her. She put it on her bedside table but couldn't sleep with it there. Even with the lights out, she kept remembering his smiling face and the inscription scrawled in the corner. "Love always, Patrick." She turned on the lights and put it back in the bottom drawer, without the letters to keep it company now. *Always*—it sounded longer than three years.

Her eyes moved to the asparagus fern, swaying at the windows. Patrick. How could she have thought she'd forget him, when she'd surrounded herself with bits and pieces of their past to keep the memory alive? But she knew she'd keep that plant and keep planting the little red berries as they ripened.

She had a hard time sleeping that night. She woke late the next morning, knowing Clare would be there to open the shop. When she arrived at work, Clare handed her a little square parcel.

"This came an hour ago. A man in a big stretch limo left it for you at nine o'clock," she said, her eyes wide in interest.

Patrick had been here, and she'd missed him! A silent, anguished howl rent her. "Thanks, Clare," she said, and was surprised to hear a normal, friendly voice come from her lips.

Elinor took the parcel into her office. She wanted to open it in private. It was wrapped in Christmas paper, covered with jolly images of Santa Claus. Inside was a brown box with a little gold seal from the Delta Arms Hotel gift shop. She opened it, curious to see what Patrick had sent her. She lifted out a little glass dome mounted on a mahogany base. The dome was filled with a clear liquid, and in it stood the tiny figures of a boy and girl. She turned it upside down, and tiny white flakes filled the water. A boy and girl, playing in the snow. She set it on her desk and watched the white flakes fall.

The touching memento unleashed a flood of memories. How like Patrick to find the perfect gift. There was no letter, just a gift card, covered with tiny writing on both sides.

Dear Ellie:
Here I go again, creating new problems for the future. I can never thank you enough, but I'll try. Have a lovely Christmas. Looking forward to New Year's.

                                        Love, Plato

PS The name has been changed to protect the innocent—or guilty, as the case may be.

She smiled and turned it over.

You're very hard to buy for, especially when Camille is too ill to go outside the hotel. Flowers would be like taking coals to Newcastle. Would you like a Gideon Bible?

That's all, but the message caught the flavor of his conversation. Light, whimsical. She could picture him, wanting to do something nice to thank her but being hampered by his cold. He was trying to ease out of this entanglement gently. Why prolong it by that New Year's visit to Rochester? She'd cancel that.

Sending him a note would be best, to save the embarrassment of him having to urge her a little. She turned the little glass dome upside down again and watched until all the snowflakes had sifted to the bottom. When Clare came knocking on the door, Elinor put the gift down and switched her mind to work. There'd be plenty of time for regrets later. A whole lifetime.

Elinor welcomed the rush of business during the next two days. After work she was busy, too, buying and wrapping presents and attending a few Christmas parties. Patrick didn't call, or if he did, she was out. He could have called the shop if he really wanted to talk to her. He knew Clare would be there if she was out, and he could leave a message. Suddenly it was Christmas Eve, and after work she exchanged gifts with Gillie. Elinor gave her a tablecloth for her hope chest, and Gillie gave her a book on orchids.

"I know you're always talking about them. Maybe someday you'll get around to trying to grow them," Gillie said.

"Thank you, Gillie. I love it."

They had a Christmas drink together, then Elinor loaded up the van and drove out to the farm. There was plenty of snow that year. It covered the roofs of the house and barns, softening their stark outlines to beauty. It lay heavy on evergreen boughs, pushing them low with its weight. Lights twinkled from the farmhouse, and with the North Star shining in a clear black sky, she could almost imagine it was the Christmas star, shining on Bethlehem. A rush of warmth and love filled her when she thought of her family, waiting. The sorrow was there, too, but she'd try to keep it at bay for this visit.

It was hard to smile and pretend everything was all right, but she made the effort for her parents' sake. With their other daughter and her husband and three grandchildren to distract them, her parents didn't notice her mood. It was nice to have little children around for Christmas. As they eagerly tore apart their presents on Christmas morning, Elinor wondered if she'd ever have children of her own to bring home for Christmas.

When these bouts of dejection became too strong to hide, Elinor went to the greenhouse and puttered with her plants. Beckie, her eldest niece, loved the greenhouse. She often went along, and Elinor enjoyed introducing her to the world of plants. Adam and Eve got plenty of attention. She went to the conservatory Christmas night, after dinner and the monumental kitchen cleanup. Patrick still hadn't called. She had thought he might call for Christmas.

As she watered her plants, she thought about that note she had to write to Patrick, canceling the New Year's visit. It was time to write it now, but it was such a sad task for Christmas night that she put it off. Maybe a telegram would be better. She wouldn't have to say much, just sorry but she couldn't make it. He'd be relieved. Yes, that's what she'd do. She'd send him a telegram on about the twenty-seventh of December, so he'd have time to get a date for whatever party he had planned. He wouldn't have any trouble.

On Monday, the twenty-seventh, she went back to work and sent the telegram from there in the afternoon. It left her feeling empty inside, the way she felt when she first left home. There was that gnawing ache of knowing that an era had ended and things would never be quite the same again. But with it came a feeling of peace that it was over. It was what Patrick really

wanted anyway. He hadn't phoned once since he left.
He would have phoned if he had any intention of
continuing this relationship. A cold didn't prevent you
from using the phone.

When she arrived home from work that evening,
there was a card from him waiting in her mailbox. She
hastened into her apartment and ripped it open before she took off her coat. It was dated Christmas Eve.

Dear Ellie:
I'm writing this from my bed. That flu bug has
me by the throat. I can hardly croak, so calling
you on the phone is out. But I can't let Christmas go by without some contact. I wish you were
here. Eagerly awaiting the New Year.

Love, Patrick

She gasped in horror at that telegram she had sent
off so recklessly. He'd have it by now. He'd think she
didn't care, that she didn't want to see him. The only
reason he hadn't called was because he couldn't. She
should have phoned; she knew he was sick. Guilt and
anguish tore at her.

She went to the phone and took up the receiver, then
set it down again, realizing she didn't know his number in Rochester. Of course, she could get it from the
operator. There couldn't be that many Barrons in
Rochester. What was his father's name? Michael, that
was it. He used to joke about Pat and Mike.

She got the number and phoned. An older woman
answered, presumably his mother. "I'm sorry,
Patrick isn't here," she said. "Is this Miss Higgins?"

"No," Elinor said, with a little sting of jealousy.

"Oh, I thought you might be calling for Mr. Firth again," she said, and Elinor's heart settled down. It was all right then; Miss Higgins was apparently Firth's secretary. How swift she was to judge Patrick! She leaped on every little thing.

"Do you know when he'll be back?" she asked.

"No, I'm afraid I don't. We may not see him for a month. He received an urgent message and went tearing out of the house two hours ago. He packed his suitcase. Something important must have come up. He mentioned visiting Mr. Firth."

"I see."

"Can I ask him to call you if I hear from him? He said he'd be calling."

But he might not call for days. "No—I—I guess not, thanks."

She hung up the phone and just stood, still wearing her coat. It must have been some political emergency that sent Patrick flying off so suddenly. Firth would probably be in Washington now. She should have asked Mrs. Barron for Patrick's phone number there.

Elinor took off her coat and put on the kettle while she pondered what to do. She wondered if Patrick had even received her telegram. She should have asked his mother if he had received her message. That telegram might have been unnecessary. If some crisis had arisen, he probably wouldn't have been at home for New Year's anyway. Maybe she should call Rochester again. . . .

Her head ached. She was ravenously hungry, quite confused and very depressed. Everything was work-

ing out all wrong. And on top of it all, Patrick wasn't
well enough to be flying about the countryside. Firth
had no concern for Patrick's health. She got out the
frying pan and cracked an egg before remembering
she'd had eggs for lunch. She'd be loaded with cho-
lesterol at this rate. Besides, she didn't want eggs
again. She wanted—not food. She wanted Patrick.
She made toast and fried the egg anyway, to assuage
the hunger pangs.

What should she do? Should she call Mrs. Barron
and get Patrick's phone number in Washington? She
couldn't call him in the middle of a political crisis.
And if there was a crisis on, he wouldn't be at his
apartment. If he hadn't received her message, he'd call
to cancel the New Year's date. And if he had ... Then
what? The next move was up to her, and it had to be
the right one. She wasn't going to rush into anything
without thinking it out carefully first.

When she had eaten and cleaned the kitchen, she
decided to pay Gillie a quick visit and see what kind of
a Christmas she'd had. Probably Luke had given her
the engagement ring she was expecting. Maybe Gillie
could help her decide what to do about Patrick. Two
heads were better than one, especially when one was
as confused as hers.

She was just brushing her hair for the visit when her
buzzer sounded. It was a continuing annoyance that
there was no intercom to let her know who was calling her. Since Tony Gower's unannounced visit, she
was leery of letting people into the building. At least
she'd soon have her new dead bolt to protect her. It
was probably some friend making a Christmas visit,

so she pushed the buzzer and waited to see who it was. She'd check through the peephole before she let anyone in.

Through the door she heard her caller bounding up the last flight of stairs, two at a time. It certainly wasn't Clare. She didn't come up at that rate. It sounded like a man. She peered through the peephole and waited till her caller came into view. When she recognized Patrick, she emitted a gasp of shocked delight and threw the door open.

"Patrick! What are you doing here?" He looked a little pale and more than a little angry.

He held out the telegram. "This is what I'm doing. Ellie, how *could* you?" He felt he had been betrayed. All during the mad drive to Delta he had been imagining Ellie into a monster. And now she stood before him, looking like a whipped child.

She looked at the telegram in chagrin, then at him. She swallowed convulsively and looked ready to cry. "Oh, you got it. I was hoping you hadn't," she said in a small voice.

Hurt and confusion lent a sharp edge to his words. "What the devil does that mean? Why did you send it if you didn't want me to read it?"

"Why don't you come in?" she said, and drew him in from the hallway.

He stood, waiting. His dark, accusing eyes demanded an explanation. "Well?"

"I can explain everything. Come and sit down."

He followed her into the living room but didn't sit down. He just stood, as if ready to bolt out in a minute. In this mood, his impetuous nature might lead him to stalk off, so she had to be careful. She took the telegram and squashed it into a ball.

"I thought you wanted out," she said simply. "When you didn't phone or anything at Christmas... Then after I had sent the telegram, I came home and found your belated Christmas card, explaining why you couldn't phone."

He looked at her in disbelief. "Wanted out? Why would I have invited you home to meet my folks if I wanted out? Ellie, I love you, and I want to marry you."

The words were like rain in a desert. "You never said so," she pointed out. Her lips wobbled, then stretched in a shy smile. "You never used the word love."

"Maybe I fought it at first. There were so many complications, and when Firth dangled that political plum in my eyes, I guess I was temporarily blinded. I knew as soon as I started seeing you again that I didn't want to lose you. I just didn't see how we could fit an early marriage into my schedule. I sound like a damned egotist—"

"No, your work's important, Patrick. Too important to risk."

"No, *you're* too important to risk. I knew for sure when I thought Gower had—I was irrational. I never want to feel that way again. I won't risk losing you, Ellie. I need you to keep me sane in this crazy business. I know I haven't been able to dance attendance on you the way a suitor should, but I had planned to put that New Year's visit to good use, making up for lost time. I thought you understood." His dark eyes examined her searchingly.

"How could I understand? You didn't even kiss me the last time we were alone."

He pulled her into his arms. "I never wanted anything so much in my life. My throat felt as if a chimney sweep was down there, reaming it out with a stiff brush. I was burning with a fever and knew I was coming down with something that was bound to be contagious. I didn't want to inflict that on you."

"It would have been better than—"

"I thought you understood. I told you." He loosened his hold and frowned in confusion. "Didn't I?"

"You mentioned not wanting to give me your cold. I guess you didn't tell me loud enough," she said.

"Didn't you get my present? I meant it as a harbinger of things to come. You, me, snow up to our eyeballs and not giving a damn. We're safe in our own private little world."

Elinor drew her lower lip between her teeth. Relief that he loved her was paramount, but there were still problems to be confronted. "Really it's two separate worlds, Patrick," she pointed out reluctantly. "We have to talk about this." She took his coat and they went to the sofa.

"I know," he said. "I've been thinking about that while I've been in bed."

She looked at him uncertainly. "I won't be much of a help to your career," she said. "I wouldn't have the least idea how to entertain politicians or—"

He took her hands in his and smiled softly. "You've done a good job of entertaining this one. What did I

know about the social scene when I started? I bought
the monkey suit and played it by ear. We'll do the
same with any social dos we have to toss. They're just
people, like us. The job really isn't about having parties, you know. And all the other new representatives'
wives will be in the same boat. I know I'd never be
anything but proud to have you by my side. That's the
least of my worries.''

He made it all sound so easy. And while she knew
it wouldn't be easy, she didn't feel it would be impossible. "What do you mean?"

"It's what I'm asking you to give up that worries me
more. I know how much your work means to you.
You *glow* when you talk about it. And I don't want to
take that away from you. But does your plant shop
really *have* to be in Delta? An awful lot of plants are
bought in Washington. Don't think of it as giving
something up but as expanding—a bigger, busier shop,
bringing more beautiful flowers to more people.''

Elinor felt a tingle of excitement at the widening of
her horizons. "I'll need a conservatory, too," she
added.

"We'll find you one. And you won't give up The
Plant Shed here completely, Ellie. If I make it, I'll be
the congressman for this district. I'll need a place in
New York State. It can be here, in Delta. That way you
can hire a manager and still keep your shop for the
future. Who knows what the future might bring?''

"I might become a whole franchise!" Ellie said ex-
citedly.

"Or I might not even get elected.''

"Yes, you will! I want that bigger, more beautiful shop in Washington, so you'll have to get elected."

"Even if I do, I might hate politics so much I leave after one term."

Ellie gave him a teasing smile. "Sure, and *I* might decide I hate growing flowers."

"We'll see. But meanwhile, we'll visit Adam and Eve and all their kin every chance we get."

"Dad can keep an eye on my greenhouse here," she said, thinking it over. "He does most of it anyway. I just go out on weekends. And maybe Clare could take over the shop. It's the only way we can be together, and *nothing* is going to keep us apart this time."

He looked at her hopefully but with still one little doubt. "You're sure you don't mind doing it?"

"I can hardly wait to expand! I offered to go with you once before, and you refused. I often wished you hadn't."

"I often wished I'd taken the job in New York. But I don't think it would have worked out then."

"Either way, one of us would have resented it."

"Will you resent coming to Washington with me now? Think carefully, darling. It's not the only option. I meant it when I said I'd quit politics. If it means losing you..."

She looked offended. "And let that toad Gower take your place?"

"Gower has accepted an offer with a private firm. Once he lost Firth's confidence, he knew his political career was sunk. It wouldn't be Gower who replaced me."

"Nobody's going to replace you. They won't move Congress here, so *you're* going to Washington, and I'm going with you. There must be fantastic flower business done in Washington, with all those parties. And I can go and see the Rose Garden at the White House. That's settled. Now, what did Firth want when he phoned you? Do you have to rush right off to Washington?"

"No, Firth's still here, in Delta. He was just checking up on my cold. How did you know he'd called?"

"I phoned, and your Mom said you got an urgent message and rushed right off."

"The urgent message was *that*," he said, pointing to the squashed telegram on the floor. "I didn't tell my parents you'd canceled, because I intended to change your mind. I guess Mom just assumed it was from Firth."

"Then you can stay here awhile?" she asked eagerly.

"Till New Year's. We have a lot to do in that short time."

"You mean—like get married?" Her eyes beamed with joy.

Patrick grasped her two hands. "The sooner the better," he said eagerly. "Things will really start heating up around the end of January. We have a wedding and a honeymoon to arrange before that. Do you think we can squeeze it all in?"

"If we start immediately."

"What are we waiting for?" he asked, and pulled her into his arms.

She lifted her face for his kiss, savoring the moment before their lips touched. She wanted to store up this memory. His lambent eyes, aglow with the urgency of love as they flickered over her face, lingering on her eyes, then moving inexorably to study her lips. The faint masculine scent of soap, mingling with resin from the Christmas tree. The gleam of colored lights over his shoulder. "Ellie, darling, I've waited so long." It was a mere echo in her ear, but it was torn from his heart, and it was the sweetest music she'd ever heard.

Her voice, when she could speak, was husky. "I love you so much." Her eyes closed, and at the same instant her lips trembled open. Then his touched them, and a flame licked through her, setting her world aglow. They were locked inside some magical sphere, as surely as the couple enclosed in the glass bubble he'd given her. The real world would impinge later, but for this exquisite moment he was hers alone.

His lips burned a fierce kiss on hers, and she looped her arms around his neck, returning every pressure. Her softer body molded itself to his form. He crushed her tighter, tighter, till she felt she was being absorbed into him. Every sense was heightened as she felt the layers of emotional protection falling away. A throbbing pulse beat inside her. It felt like the rhythm of the universe, or love. She felt his tongue stroking at her lips, and when he claimed the intimacy of her mouth, a sighing moan, quiet as the breath of angels, hung on the air.

This is how it would be, in the near future. Stolen moments, but all the sweeter for having to wait.

After a long kiss, he released her and got up. He went to his overcoat and came back, carrying a little box. "Merry Christmas," he said, and handed it to her. "I'm afraid it isn't wrapped. I bought it in Rochester before I left, hoping to lure you with diamonds if pleading didn't work."

Her fingers trembled as she opened it. In the satin lining, a small, perfect flower of diamonds reposed. At the center of the flower was one ruby. "It's beautiful, Patrick! Where did you find such a lovely thing?"

He slid it out and put it on her trembling finger. "Lady Luck was with me. The jeweler must have had you in mind when he created it."

She admired it a moment, then looked up guiltily. "I didn't get you anything! This is two presents you've given me, and I didn't get you anything."

He kissed her hand, gazing into her eyes. "You've given me the best present of all. Love. You've given me everything."

She smiled through a mist of tears. "Not everything. I still have a lot to give. Would you like some maté?"

He lifted a black brow and grinned. "Well, it's not exactly what I had in mind, but it'll do for starters."

*   *   *   *   *

Silhouette Desire®

1989
IS THE YEAR
OF THE MAN!

What makes a romance? A special man, of course, and Silhouette Desire cele-brates that fact with *twelve* of them! From Mr. January to Mr. December, every month has a tribute to the Silhouette Desire hero—our **MAN OF THE MONTH!**

Sexy, macho, charming, irritating . . . irresistible! Nothing can stop these men from sweeping you away. Created by some of your favorite authors, each man is custom-made for pleasure—*reading* pleasure—so don't miss a single one.

Mr. January is Blake Donavan in RELUCTANT FATHER by Diana Palmer
Mr. February is Hank Branson in THE GENTLEMAN INSISTS by Joan Hohl
Mr. March is Carson Tanner in NIGHT OF THE HUNTER by Jennifer Greene
Mr. April is Slater McCall in A DANGEROUS KIND OF MAN by Naomi Horton
Mr. May is Luke Harmon in VENGEANCE IS MINE by Lucy Gordon
Mr. June is Quinn McNamara in IRRESISTIBLE by Annette Broadrick

And that's only the half of it—
so get out there and find your man!

Silhouette Desire's

MAN OF THE MONTH . . .

MOM-1

COMING IN APRIL

NAVY BLUES
Debbie Macomber

Between the devil and the deep blue sea...

At Christmastime, Lieutenant Commander Steve Kyle finds his heart anchored by the past, so he vows to give his ex-wife wide berth. But Carol Kyle is quaffing milk and knitting tiny pastel blankets with a vengeance. She's determined to have a baby, and only one man will do as father-to-be—the only man she's ever loved...her own bullheaded ex-husband! Can the wall of bitterness protecting Steve's battered heart possibly withstand the hurricane force of his Navy wife's will?

You met Steve and Carol in NAVY WIFE (Special Edition #494)—you'll cheer for them in NAVY BLUES (Special Edition #518). (And as a bonus for NAVY WIFE fans, newlyweds Rush and Lindy Callaghan reveal a surprise of their own....)

Each book stands alone—together they're Debbie Macomber's most delightful duo to date! Don't miss

NAVY BLUES
Available in April,
only in *Silhouette Special Edition*.
Having the "blues" was never
so much fun!

SE518-1